PHOEBE'S PROMISE

Oregon Sky Book One

KAY P. DAWSON

Phoebe's Promise: Oregon Sky Book One
Print version
© Copyright 2022 (As Revised) Kay P. Dawson

CKN Christian Publishing
An Imprint of Wolfpack Publishing
5130 S. Fort Apache Rd. 215-380
Las Vegas, NV 89148

cknchristianpublishing.com

Print ISBN 978-1-63977-221-6

PHOEBE'S PROMISE

This book is dedicated to my aunt Phoebe - one of my biggest fans. You never let me believe that my writing was just good enough...in your eyes (which I always knew were maybe just a bit biased), my books were the "best you had ever read." Thank you for helping me to believe I could really do this.

Thank you also to my family who has had to endure me talking endlessly about the Oregon Trail and live with the maps and books spread all over the house.

I also want to send out a big thank you to Melissa Lark Scott who came up with the great name for the villain in the book, Titus Cain. (And, a special mention to the real Titus Cain - thanks for the inspiration ;)

*And, of course - thank you **to you** for taking the time to read my book! I hope you enjoy reading it as much as I enjoyed writing it.*

CHAPTER 1

"I don't know how you're going to pull this off, Phoebe. There is no way anyone is going to believe you're a man."

Phoebe clenched her hands tighter on the reins, staring ahead at the scene before her. Everywhere she looked, she saw the white of the covered wagons. Men were walking around, talking, and lifting supplies into the wagons.

There were women, too. But most of the women who would be making the trek across the country were married, many with children hanging from their skirts.

Phoebe watched them closely as they soothed crying babies, shook clothing out of the back of the wagons to get the dust out, and crouched down tending to the meal that would feed their families tonight before the start of their long journey in the morning.

They all wore long dresses covered with aprons and many had bonnets on their heads. Some women had their bonnets hanging off the back of their necks as they worked to ready the wagons.

"Grace, this is what we have to do. Luke wouldn't send us here if he didn't think it would be safe for us. We have to do it; you know there's no other option for us."

She tried to calm her own nerves by soothing her sister's worries but inside, her stomach was in knots, threatening to give her away.

It was hard to believe that just a day ago, her brother Luke had sent them on with the wagon full of supplies to make a trip across the country. He was heading back to St. Louis to deal with their uncle, Ivan, a man they suspected of having a hand in their father's death.

She felt a twinge in her chest as she thought of her pa. He had died heroically during the great fire that had erupted in the city almost a year ago. He'd gone into their burning mercantile to save a baby their uncle had said was still inside.

But after the fire was out, they found no sign of a baby ever having been in there.

Her ma died from cholera just a month before their father's death, so she and Grace were left in the care of their uncle until their brother Luke came home. He'd fought with their father a year before and left, saying he was going looking for gold.

When he finally came home, Phoebe told him her suspicions and let him know her fears about her uncle. He wasted no time getting them away from there.

She tried to keep her anger toward her brother in check. Not only had he left them to deal with the death of their parents alone, while he went on adventures all over the country, but then he wouldn't listen to reason when she tried telling him she could handle her uncle. She wanted to help prove that he'd killed her pa.

Now, here she was sitting on a loaded wagon, about to set off on a trail across the country with only her sister and a bunch of strangers.

Except, of course, for Colton Wallace, the man she had to find. Her brother had sent a letter explaining everything and told her to find him and give it to him. He promised her the man would take care of them.

She didn't have much to go on, other than he was tall, and had dark hair and blue eyes. She figured there were likely a hundred men in their company fitting that description.

"Just sit here with the wagon and I will be right back." She hooked the reins around the front of the wagon. The oxen pawed the ground, then bent their heads to see what grass they could find to graze on.

Her sister grabbed her arm before she could get down from the seat. Phoebe stopped and stared into fearful green eyes. "Please don't be too long!" Her sister pleaded.

Grace was only twelve years old and Phoebe felt terrible leaving her alone for even a moment. She was scared herself and she was six years older.

"I won't be long, I promise." She reached out and patted her sister's hand, trying to offer her some reassurance. All around them, voices were shouting out orders and people were running wild getting everything ready for the trip ahead.

The truth was her own body trembled with fear but she would never let her sister know that. Right now, she was all Grace had to depend on and she wasn't going to let her down. Luke believed in her and she was going to prove his confidence in her wasn't misplaced.

She wasn't used to wearing pants and the boots on her feet were hot and uncomfortable, not to mention a size too big. But in their haste to leave the city, the ill-fitting clothes and boots were all they could find.

She tugged her jacket tighter around her shoulders, not wanting anyone to see her curves even though she had wrapped those same curves so tight with fabric, there wasn't much chance of that happening anyway.

The hat she wore was a bit big but she was at least able to pull her hair up tight beneath it. She knew if anything gave her away, it would be her hair. Someone once told her it was the color of the brightest sunset or as her uncle said, the color of the devil's own eyes.

Luke told her to cut it off but she hadn't been able to do it. Now though, as she glanced around her and saw the reality of her situation, she realized she should have listened to her brother. She couldn't risk getting caught.

Two women alone on a wagon train was too tempting a target for unscrupulous men.

"Hmph! Watch where you're going there, young man! You can get yourself run over if you don't keep your eyes in front of you." A burly man with a grey beard down to his chest bumped into her, almost knocking her over as she came around a wagon.

"Sorry." She tried to keep her voice low, looking toward the ground in an attempt to hide her face.

Walking as quickly as she could, she gripped the letter in her hand tighter. She weaved in and out between wagons, sidestepping scampering, excited children, while narrowly managing to escape being stepped on by an unyoked ox.

Fear kept her moving forward. She needed to find the man her brother had sent her to find. If her brother trusted him, she knew he was someone who'd help her get her sister to safety.

Phoebe spotted a man near a small group of wagons, shouting orders from atop a horse. She stopped to take a better look. Her brother said he could be a bit intimidating in his manners, but he assured her he wasn't half as ornery as he let everyone believe he was. Her brother had been trying to make her feel better but she knew he was also likely trying to warn her about the man she needed to trust.

"Take that wagon and move it over there out of the way! And get those kids out from under our feet before someone gets themselves killed!" The man's voice boomed across the space between the wagons.

The man hopped down, reaching out to pull a small child out of harm's way as a wagon rolled past.

As she watched, the child's mother ran over to take her son from the man. Phoebe couldn't hear what he said to her but she nodded and then practically dragged the child back to their wagon.

Phoebe was so wrapped up in watching the woman and child she nearly jumped from her boots when she noticed the man was now standing right in front of her.

"Where are your parents?" He was scowling at her. She hoped this wasn't Colton Wallace.

Swallowing hard, she lowered her voice to speak.

"Don't have any folks here with me. It's just me and my little sister."

The man raised an eyebrow, then whipped his hat off his head and swept his hair back out of his eyes before slapping it back on his head. She noticed it was in need of a cut and the color was as black as coal. His eyes were bluer than the sky above them.

He had to be the man her brother sent her to find. He didn't look happy to be left in charge of a young man and his sister, so she was sure he'd be even less happy when he discovered the truth.

"Do you realize the extent of the journey we have ahead of us through the roughest stretches of land you will ever see in your life? This isn't going to be a two or three-day ride. So if you think you are going to try doing a trip like this on your own, with a younger sister to take care of, then I question your sanity. I can't tell you no but I can tell you right now I don't have the time or inclination to be spending the entire trip looking after a boy and his sister." His jaw was clenched tight and she could see the muscles in his neck moving as he tried to control his anger.

Lifting her chin a little higher, she thought she saw a flicker of his eyes as he creased his eyebrows and she saw him lean in closer to her. Determined not to back away from his scrutiny, she looked him straight in the eye. "Are you Colton Wallace?"

He didn't move a muscle for what seemed like forever, then slowly he nodded his head. "I am. And, I didn't just fall off the turnip wagon. So do you want to tell me who you are and exactly why you are dressed as a boy?"

Thrusting the letter into his hands, she didn't say a word until he finally lowered his gaze and opened the envelope. She watched him as he read the words her brother had hastily scrawled onto the page. Colton slowly lifted his face, his eyes holding her in place.

Her heart pounded in her chest but she kept her gaze on his, not prepared to back down.

Grabbing her by the arm, he dragged her to a tree off to the side of the gathered wagons.

"Get your hands off me you big oaf!" She was tired, hungry, and just as upset about the situation she found herself in as he was. If he thought he was going to toss her around like a sack of flour, he had another thing coming.

"Quiet!" He stopped and turned to face her again. "Now, do you mind telling me what the hell is going on? If you expect me to believe you are Luke Hamilton's sister and that he wants me to take you all the way across the country with nothing more than a letter telling me so, you had better start talking!"

CHAPTER 2

His nerves were stretched as tight as they could go and he was trying his hardest not to lose his temper. The stress of the day had worn on him as he readied the wagon train to start off in the morning. News like this wasn't welcome at this point.

The moment she lifted her eyes and glared at him, he had known she was a woman and not the boy she was pretending to be. The letter from his friend said he needed Colton to look after his younger sisters until he could join them, hopefully soon. But he hadn't been sure how long he would be and he thought dressing his oldest sister as a boy would help keep her safer on the trail. A young woman without a chaperone was too much tempta- tion for the single men, especially when they appeared as pretty as he suspected she did without the boy clothes.

He noticed her swallow hard and wondered if she'd turn around and run away from him. He almost hoped she would.

"My brother is Luke Hamilton, and he assured me you were someone he would trust with his life." Her eyes flashed with anger. "However, from what I have seen, I'm not sure why he would consider a man as abrasive as you a friend." He heard her voice catch as she spoke and he realized she was trying hard to put on a brave face in a situation that was obviously beyond her control.

Pulling his hat from his head again, he slapped it against his thighs, trying to get his own frustration under control.

He whipped out the letter and reread the words carefully.

Colton,

I am trusting you with the only remaining family I have, my sisters Phoebe and Grace. I returned from our travels to find my mother dead from cholera and my father killed in a fire. I have my suspicions that it was our uncle who is responsible for his death and I intend to find out the truth.

Since I was gone, my sisters were forced to live with my uncle. He has tried to harm both of them, and I can't have them here while I do what I need to do. I am left with no choice but to get them as far away from him as I can.

I know it is asking a great favour of you to take them with you but I will do everything in my power to join up with you along the way.

If, however, I can't catch up with the train, I am asking you to take them with you to your family in Oregon until I can come for them. I will explain everything then.

Phoebe is tough as nails and she will do her part to get them both to the other end of the trail, with or without my help. I've dressed her as a boy hoping to keep her safe along the way, although I suspect it will be difficult to keep that hidden for the entire journey, which I am sure by that time, you will be able to handle.

There is no one else I would trust with something as precious as my sisters and I am hoping you will do me this favor. I will forever be indebted to you.

Luke

Colton stared down at the letter, listening to the sounds of the people milling around, preparing their wagons. Dust settled around him as people and animals moved throughout the camp readying everything for the morning.

"So, why didn't your brother bring you here himself, instead of sending you to me, with only a letter asking me to do something as foolhardy as dragging you two girls across the country with me?"

She crossed her arms in front of her and, by the way she was clenching her jaw, he could tell she was biting her tongue hard to keep from giving away her own frustration. "He said he knew if he came, you would argue and likely wouldn't agree to help. He sent us on our own with a letter knowing you'd be unable to say no." She hadn't even tried to lie.

His eyes fell to the letter in his hands. He had to get his anger under control.

"Well, I don't see any other option. I can't very well leave you sitting here on your own." He lifted his gaze, finding himself caught in her angry stare. Her arms were crossed in front of her and she wasn't moving a muscle. If he didn't know better, she was daring him to say he wouldn't take her.

"I assure you, I'm not thrilled with the prospect of spending the next few weeks traveling all the way across the country, wearing cumbersome clothes that are two sizes too big. I haven't been given any choice in the matter either, my brother practically dragged us here. I tried to assure him I could handle my uncle as I have *already* been doing since my parents died. The only reason I didn't fight him more was because I needed to get my sister away from our uncle." He watched her shoulders hitch as she took a deep breath. "So, if you're worried about me being a burden, I promise you I will do my share of the work and you won't be bothered with me or my sister any more than you would with any of the others in this wagon train."

Colton couldn't take his eyes off hers. He found himself actually believing she could make this trip on her own.

He and Luke Hamilton had been through a great deal together and he knew he'd never betray his friend's trust. But he sure didn't like the thought of having to keep two women safe for the next few months. The risks they'd face as they moved west were more than any of them could imagine.

"So, I'm guessing you are Phoebe?"

She nodded.

"And, what provisions did you bring for the trip? I hope your brother thought to provide for your needs and didn't leave me to do that as well." He was irritated and he knew he sounded like a petulant child but he didn't care.

Phoebe stood completely still in front of him.

"So Mr. Wallace, does that mean you will take us with you?" She appeared relieved even though she didn't seem happy to be here, either. Her face was dirty; there were deep circles under her eyes and she seemed too grown up to be so young. She'd obviously carried a great burden on her shoulders—just getting her and her sister to the wagon train on her own must've taken its toll.

He started walking back toward the wagons. "Yes. Your brother is a friend so I won't turn my back on his request to help. But I'm not going to like it." He didn't know why added that last bit.

He turned back to find Phoebe trying to keep pace in boots that were too big. He ground his teeth together, willing his anger to calm.

"And, before we leave tomorrow, I'm taking you to the closest mercantile and getting you a pair of boots that fit properly! How did you plan on walking thousands of miles in those boots?"

He turned and started to walk away but before he could move three steps, something hit him square on the shoulder. He reached up to rub the spot where he'd been hit, then looked down to see one of the boots in question lying beside him on the ground.

Slowly, he bent down to pick it up, then turned back to face the woman who was now glaring at him, wearing only one boot. Her hands were in tight fists at her side and her chest was heaving as she breathed.

He raised an eyebrow.

She walked over, calmly took the boot from his hand, put it back on, then walked right past him— as though nothing had just happened.

He suddenly tasted dirt and realized his mouth was hanging open as he watched her walk away. " I am quite sure my brother thought of everything; however, you are welcome to come take a look for yourself." He watched her retreating back and had no choice but to follow her.

Catching up with her, he grabbed her arm and bent low enough that only she could hear his next words. "I am the captain of this wagon train, so you will not do anything like that again. If you do, you will have to face the same consequences as any other who would dare to challenge me. Do I make myself clear?"

She squinted as she returned his gaze. Her eyes brightened when she was angry.

"Perfectly." And with that, she turned and walked away again.

CHAPTER 3

P hoebe gripped the reins with all of her strength, trying to control the team of oxen pulling the wagon through deep ruts. She'd never been on a bumpier ride in her life. She glanced to her sister. Grace was gripping the outside seat handle and holding the front bar of the wagon with her other hand, desperately trying not to bounce right off the seat.

They'd set off that morning almost before the sun started peeking over the horizon. Last night, Colton gathered everyone, telling them to be ready at first light. That meant having their meal and cleaning up, then loading the wagon and hitching the team in the dark.

That morning, she and Grace had worked together to make a meal of bacon and bread, and cups of black coffee, to fortify them for the day ahead. She'd noticed Colton moving from wagon to wagon, checking on everything. When he got to theirs, he didn't even try to hide the fact he'd have rather turned and run the other direction. She knew he didn't think she could handle this on her own and, truth be known, she was worried about it herself.

But because he made her feel more of a burden to him than any of the others, it strengthened her determination not to ask him for any help.

She'd smiled up at him with the most insincere smile she could manage and offered him a bite to eat and some coffee. He gruffly refused, asking them if they had everything else ready, reminding them they had little time left to have the wagon packed and the team hooked up.

It had felt so good to sweep her hand in the direction of the team, showing him the wagon was already hitched and ready to leave.

Of course, he'd gone over to check everything for himself anyway, then merely nodded at her before moving to the next wagon.

She smiled even now, thinking about it. She wasn't fooling herself into believing she wouldn't need any help from him during the rest of the journey but that one small victory definitely boosted her spirits.

"Oh Phoebe! I don't think I will be able to stand this the rest of the way!" Poor Grace was so small, she didn't have the weight to hold herself in the seat.

"Would you like to get out and walk beside the wagon? I see quite a few women doing that. Maybe when we get a little further onto the trail things will smooth out a bit." She doubted it but didn't let her sister know that. She was ready to get down and just lead the team from the ground.

"I think I'd rather walk. Can you stop for a minute to let me off?" Grace turned to Phoebe as she asked. They weren't going fast at all, so those walking were able to keep up easily. But she knew it was dangerous for a woman with skirts to jump from a moving wagon, so she pulled on the reins to bring them to a stop.

The others on the trail were moving slow enough that stopping for a few minutes wasn't going to leave them behind. Her hope of the wagon train moving quickly had disappeared after only an hour on the trail. What she imagined about the trip was nowhere near what she was living.

She stepped down to stretch her legs and give her back a rest. As soon as her second foot was on the ground and she turned to walk away from the wagon, a horse stopped right in front of her. She squinted up and saw Colton scowling down at her.

"We'll be stopping for lunch just up ahead. Why are you stopping now? Do you have something wrong with your wagon?" He sounded irritated again which Phoebe was beginning to believe was the only temperament he had.

"Don't you ever smile?" She walked toward the back of the wagon, pressing on her lower back to ease some of the knots. "We are just stopping long enough for Grace to get down and walk. The jarring of the wagon is a bit harsh for someone as small as she is." Grace came around the wagon to stand beside her.

"I'm sorry, Mr. Wallace. I asked her to stop because I was having some trouble holding on to the wagon with all of the bouncing." Grace could obviously sense how irritated Colton was with Phoebe, having witnessed the way they spoke to each other. She was always the one who wanted to make things right with people, the one who tried to smooth things over.

The exact opposite of Phoebe.

"Call me Colton." He nodded down at Grace, then tipped his hat toward her. "Walking alongside the wagon will make things a lot easier for you. Not so much bumping." Phoebe was sure she caught a smile on his face as he kicked in his heels and rode away.

She wasn't sure why she was so irritated that he could smile for her sister but seemed to save his sourness for her.

PHOEBE'S LEGS crumpled beneath her when she finally reached her sister who was working on their evening meal. It felt like days had passed since they left that morning.

She knew she had to help her sister with the cooking but her whole body felt like it weighed ten times more than normal. She felt every bone in her body and every muscle screamed in pain.

But even as she sat there, she noticed Colton making his way toward her. Determined not to let him see how exhausted she was, she jumped up to help with the meal.

"Did you get the oxen unhitched and settled for the night?"

"Yes, I moved them over with the others." She had followed the other men who were leading theirs toward a spot just off to the side of the camp. There were armed men who would take turns guarding them and she knew since everyone still thought she was a boy, she would have to take a turn one of the nights.

She poured a cup of coffee, then held it out to him. He contemplated for a moment, seeming like he would refuse but he finally took it from her hand. His fingers grazed hers and she quickly wrenched her hand away, hoping he didn't notice how it affected her.

She poured herself a cup then returned her gaze

to Colton, who was staring at her with that same scowl.

Tilting her head to the side, she couldn't resist. "Is it just me you save your ornery side for? I can't imagine how my brother could've tolerated being around someone as unpleasant as you."

She brushed past him to sit on one of the crates she'd unloaded. She sat down, now uncaring if he noticed how tired she was.

He walked over to her, taking a seat on another crate. Phoebe noticed that Grace kept glancing over nervously, most likely watching to see if they were going to fight.

"Here Mr. Wallace...I mean Colton. Would you like some bacon and fresh biscuits?" Her sister shot Phoebe a look as she walked over, silently telling her to be nice.

"Oh no, that's fine Grace. You didn't need to make me anything." Colton shifted uncomfortably.

"It's no trouble. You've been asked to look after us, so the least we can do is prepare some meals for you. Luke made sure we had enough provisions to be able to repay your kindness while we are in your care."

Phoebe couldn't help but choke on her coffee as Grace talked about repaying his kindness. He certainly wasn't showing *her* kindness at all. In fact, it was as though he went out of his way to be anything but kind to her.

Grace and Colton turned her direction as she sputtered, the coffee dribbling from her mouth. Grace looked mortified but Phoebe saw the corner of Colton's mouth almost turn up into a smile.

"Well, since you were so kind to ask, I reckon I'd love to have some of this fine food you're offering, Grace." The smile he sent in Phoebe's direction made her want to throw the rest of the coffee in his face. It was obvious he was only staying to annoy her.

Grace glared a silent warning and then handed her a plate.

Colton took his hat off as Grace handed him his plate, wasting no time in throwing food in his mouth in hunger. What she wouldn't give to take her own hat off, letting her hair loose to cool down a bit. Wearing a hat in this dust all day made her head incredibly itchy. But she knew she couldn't dare risk anyone seeing her full head of hair.

"The men have been talking about shifts for guarding the animals." He lifted his head and stared at her as he popped the last bit of biscuit in his mouth. "Let me know when they ask you to do a shift. I'll do it for you."

She clenched her teeth. "I'm capable of guarding a herd of animals for a few hours."

He kept his gaze on hers, then he dropped his shoulders, lowered his head, and rubbed his eyes. "Phoebe, I have no doubt you can. But I'm asking you to let me help you. I don't think you realize just how fast something, or someone, can sneak up on you, and being in a middle of a bunch of stampeding animals isn't where you want to be. I'm merely looking out for Luke's family. So, whether you want my help or not, you'll be getting it."

With that, he stood up and handed his plate back to Grace. "Thank you for the delicious food, Grace. It is much appreciated." Then he turned toward Phoebe and waited for what seemed like a very long time before saying, "Good night, Pete." He said it loud enough for others to hear, then grinned as he turned and walked away.

Phoebe cringed at the use of the name they had decided to use for her. He knew she didn't like it but she had no choice. Scowling at his retreating back, she resisted the temptation to throw her empty cup at it.

CHAPTER 4

Colton and a few of the other men rode ahead of the wagons, scouting to make sure the trail was clear of any trouble. He knew he had to keep his head on the job but his mind kept going back to the woman who seemed determined to make every day a challenge.

He wasn't sure why he felt so angry around her.

If Luke had been with them, he never would have agreed to it, no matter how much he felt he owed their brother. He traveled this trail as a young boy and he knew too well the dangers that lay ahead. Keeping his eye on two lone women on a wagon train wasn't in his plans.

He'd been hired to escort this company of wagons to the Oregon Territory safely. Having to watch over Phoebe and Grace made it harder for him to ensure they all made it.

They'd been traveling for a few days and every time he encountered Phoebe, she went out of her way to make him angry. If she wasn't throwing shoes at him, she was arguing with him about everything.

The third night out, it had been her turn to do a night watch for a few hours until the switch just past midnight. She'd been adamant she was going to do it and, if he hadn't have known better, he'd thought she had agreed to do it just to rile him.

He said he was going to help and they argued. She declared that she didn't need his help, saying it would seem strange for the captain to help one man and no one else.

He reluctantly agreed to let her do it. But he sat watch just out of her sight so she wouldn't know he'd been there.

"Captain! There are some mean looking clouds over to the west!" One of the lead men pulled his horse up beside him.

Colton hadn't even noticed the skies, being so wrapped up in his thoughts. Another reason having two women in his care made his job more difficult.

He glanced up at the dark clouds and felt the wind picking up.

"Quick! We have to stop the wagons and pen the animals in the middle to avoid any stampeding if the storm gets bad." He turned his horse and raced back toward the wagons making their way across the open fields. He knew how bad these spring storms could be, so he needed to get them prepared to stand against whatever was coming.

He automatically scanned for the small figure driving the wagon near the front. When he spotted her, he kicked his horse in her direction.

"There's a storm coming. We're going to pull the wagons into a circle and try to keep the animals inside to avoid them getting away if spooked. Stop your wagon here while I go ahead and tell the others."

He didn't even give her time to argue before moving on to the wagon behind her. James and Susan O'Hara were an older couple with no children and Colton knew the man would be able to help Phoebe and Grace if necessary.

"James. Bad storm headed our way. We're going to circle the wagons. I am going to go on ahead and tell the others. Can you help young Pete and his sister if they look like they're having any trouble?"

The older man nodded as Colton moved on to the next wagon. The other men who'd been out scouting ahead were racing to the other wagons and, within just a few minutes, the wagons were moving into a circle formation. The extra livestock were herded into the center.

The canvas on the wagons bowed under the strong winds and Colton felt the first drops of rain hit his face as he rode around the perimeter of the circle, making sure everything was secure.

He approached Phoebe's wagon and scanned the area to make sure she'd managed to tie everything down. The rain started coming down in fierce streams, pouring off the brim of his hat. Just as he felt the first hard pellet of hail hit his face, he noticed a small figure trying to undo the crate carrying two chickens she had tied to the back of her wagon.

Jumping down from his horse, he led it over and tied it to the back of the wagon.

"What are you doing? Get inside before you get blown away!" He grabbed her arm and dragged her toward the opening in the canvas. He noticed Grace peering out, her eyes showing her fear.

"No!" Phoebe yanked her arm free from his grip and, without even looking at him, went back to undoing the leather straps holding the cage. "I can't leave them out here!"

He stared at her in confusion. Surely she wasn't serious. "Phoebe! They are chickens. You can get hurt out here in this storm. Now get in the wagon or I will put you in myself."

He couldn't believe she'd be this careless over a couple of chickens. The hail was coming down hard, hurting him where it contacted his skin, so he knew she was hurting too. The animals in the makeshift corral were uneasy and he worried she'd get trampled if they decided to run.

She had one of the straps undone by now and the

cage was teetering at a dangerous angle. He glanced at her face and recognized the determined set of her jaw. She lifted her gaze to his. He could see she was scared, but not about to leave the chickens out here.

Growling low in his throat, he pushed her aside and swiftly undid the other strap, grabbing hold of the handle, and pushing it into the wagon. He turned to grab her arm to throw her in behind the cage. Just as he reached out for her, a gust of wind belted past them, ripping the hat from her head.

Her gaze met his with a fear so strong it felt like a swift kick to the gut. He saw the mass of hair fall around her shoulders. At the same time, he saw some of the men racing from wagon to wagon, tying down straps and tightening up the canvas flapping in the wind.

He grabbed her around the waist and threw her unceremoniously into the back of the wagon, trying to shield her from sight.

He looked around, hoping no one else saw her hair, but with the rain and hail pouring out of the sky, he couldn't see clearly. He raced to her hat, which was settled against the wheel of a neighboring wagon, and grabbed it.

As he turned, he noticed Titus Cain standing beside his wagon. The man had been butting heads with Colton since the day they left, not happy about following orders. He was one of the many single men on the wagon train, heading west to claim some land to start a family of his own.

The look on his face left no doubt about what he'd seen.

Colton leaped up on the ledge of Phoebe's wagon and threw aside the canvas. The women were huddled together in the far corner with the chickens in the cage beside them. Grace had tucked her head under Phoebe's shoulder and Phoebe's head was bent down, whispering to her sister while she stroked the back of her head.

The scene before him stopped him from saying the words he was about to say.

Phoebe lifted her wet head to meet his stare. Her red hair was tumbling around her shoulders, and he was sure he'd never seen a woman so beautiful in his life.

Shaking his head to clear his thoughts, he sat down and turned to tie up the opening against the wind tossing the wagon back and forth like a ship on the sea.

He could see the women were scared even if Phoebe would never admit it.

"Did anyone see?" she quietly asked. He almost couldn't hear her above the creaking boards of the wagon.

Pulling his own hat off his head, he nodded. "Not sure who else but I'm pretty certain Titus

Cain may have noticed." He watched her reaction as she understood the meaning of his words.

Everyone on the wagon train knew of Titus Cain's reputation even after just a few days on the trail. She was smart enough to realize he would likely cause trouble over what he saw.

Phoebe turned her head to the side wall of the wagon and Colton noticed her swallow hard.

"What happened, Phoebe?" Grace lifted her frightened eyes to look at her sister.

Phoebe smiled down at her. "It's not a big deal, really. My hat blew off in the wind."

Grace gasped then glanced over at Colton. "Oh no!"

"It's all right, Grace. I will take care of it. Truth is, I'm surprised we were able to hide your sister's true identity for this long. Being in close company with this many people on a difficult trail doesn't make it easy to keep secrets." He was trying to soothe Grace who looked like she was about to cry.

Phoebe was watching him. "So, now what should we do?"

Colton wished he knew himself. He did know that his work looking after the two girls was about to get a whole lot more difficult. It was one thing to protect them from the dangers of the trail but now he had the extra worry of keeping them safe from those who might think to take advantage of them.

As the wind raged on outside, he thought he

heard the rain let up a little. He hoped the storm didn't damage anything. He knew the trail ahead was going to be even tougher to navigate with mud as thick as molasses and skittish animals.

He tried to hold his anger in check. "What were you thinking? Why were you so insistent on bringing those chickens inside? If you would've just got in the wagon like I told you, we wouldn't be dealing with this now."

As he watched her, he noticed her eyes go from fear to anger. Her jaw clenched together as she glared at him. "I couldn't just leave them out there in the rain like that!" She spoke as though *he* was the one being thick-headed and should have known that already.

He stared at her, realizing she was completely serious. She was the kind of woman who would risk her own life to help chickens. He shook his head.

"Phoebe. Chickens can be replaced. What you did was put your own life at risk and now, because of it, we will have to deal with the consequences of others realizing you and your sister are two women out here on their own."

"Well, I wasn't going to leave them out there to die. So, we will just have to come up with a plan for dealing with the others knowing I'm a woman." She was sitting up tall, still holding an arm around her sister who was quietly listening to them talk. "Besides, I was tired of wearing these boots. And, how you men can stand wearing these pants, scratching at your legs all day long, I will never know!"

For the first time in a very long time, Colton found himself at a loss for words as he sat gaping incredulously at the woman in front of him. Her hair was drying in curls and flying in every direction.

Now that she'd be wearing appropriate garb for women, he knew he was in for even more trouble.

And the look on her face dared him to complain about it.

CHAPTER 5

The beating of the rain finally stopped and, even though the wind was still shaking the wagon, the strength of it had ebbed. She heard people walking around outside, checking for damage, cleaning up and talking with their neighbors.

She tugged the hairbrush through her curls, fighting with the knots that formed from being tucked under the hat and then being whipped around in the wind. She thought about Colton and yanked even harder at her hair, wincing when the brush got tangled.

He was always angry with her. She couldn't have just left the chickens out there in that storm. It wasn't her fault she had a soft spot for animals. She couldn't leave them to suffer even if they were just chickens.

She knew he was mad and she felt bad that he was now going to have to deal with everyone knowing their secret but, the truth was, she was glad she didn't have to pretend anymore.

She hated having to keep her hair tucked up under the hat all day. And, she wanted to wear comfortable clothes.

But Colton was acting like she'd set fire to the wagons. She didn't mean to let her secret out so soon, and she had ensured him she could handle the advances of any men who might take advantage of her situation.

He'd just shook his head again, thrust his hat back onto his head, and ordered her to stay in the wagon until he had a chance to see what damage had been done, to both the wagons and to her secret.

After Colton jumped from the wagon, she quickly changed into dry clothes, relishing the feeling of being back in one of her dresses. She was glad to put her own boots on, sighing as the soft leather folded around her blistered and sore feet.

Pulling her hair back, she tucked some pins in to keep it out of her face. She searched her traveling chest for her favorite bonnet. No more heavy hat sitting on her head.

She felt bad for her relief at getting caught. She knew it was going to cause a lot more work for

Colton but she tried not to let herself think about it.

"Phoebe, what's going to happen now?" Grace's voice trembled as she spoke. Her younger sister was sitting on a crate near the back of the wagon, hands folded in her lap. Her big green eyes showed her fear.

Phoebe stood and moved to sit down beside her. She put her arm around Grace's shoulders and pulled her sister in close. Sometimes, she forgot how young Grace was and that she was completely relying on Phoebe to take care of her. She had no one else.

After everything her sister had been through, Phoebe needed to remember the reason she was even on this wagon train in the first place. If it had just been her, her brother wouldn't have been able to convince her to go.

But she was doing this for Grace.

"Don't worry, peanut, we will be fine." When Grace was upset, Phoebe would use the name her father had always called her...Peanut. It soothed them both, almost as though their pa was there, putting his arms around them. "Luke knew my secret wouldn't stay hidden for long, anyway. He'd just hoped it would last long enough for the train to get far enough along that our being here wouldn't be able to be questioned."

"Mr. Wallace is so upset. What if he makes us go

back?" Her voice sounded so scared it tore at Phoebe's heart. She didn't care what happened with Colton or the men in the wagon train. She would never make Grace go near their uncle again. Even if she had to take them the rest of the way to Oregon on her own.

"I'm not going to make you go back, Grace." Both girls jumped at Colton's voice coming from the opening at the back of the wagon. The wind made the canvas slap against the wood so loudly, they hadn't heard him approach.

"I gave my word to get you both safely away from whatever your brother was trying to protect you from back home. Until he meets up with us, you can trust that I'll do everything I can to ensure no harm comes to you." Phoebe noticed a smile slowly make its way across Grace's face.

She hadn't seen her sister smile in a long time. Looking up at Colton, she offered him a smile to thank him for helping make her sister feel safe. For the first time, she noticed the kindness in his eyes. He hid it well, when he was barking out orders for the wagons, but she sensed he was a man she could trust even if she didn't always agree with him.

He appeared surprised when she smiled at him and it almost made her laugh to watch the confusion on his face. He, obviously, wasn't expecting it. What he probably didn't realize was that now, in her own comfortable clothes, she was feeling much more agreeable.

He put his hand out to her. "Let's get you out here and introduce you properly to the others and set down the rules for how they will treat you and your sister for the remainder of this trip." Stepping down from the wagon, Phoebe felt the sting of the wind. Even though it had died down from the storm it had been, it was still cold and wet.

She watched while he reached in and helped her sister down, taking her hand and smiling at her like she was a princess. Even though she knew her sister was nervous about what was about to happen, when Grace looked at Colton, it seemed to give her strength.

Phoebe turned and noticed everyone milling around, obviously waiting for orders from Colton.

Once they caught sight of her and Grace, everyone seemed to stop. They weren't a large outfit, perhaps about thirty wagons, so most of the people could recognize each other. They knew this wasn't the Pete they'd known since the beginning of the journey.

Phoebe lifted her chin and Colton came to stand beside her. Grace stayed back near the wagon, wringing her hands in front of her.

"This is Phoebe Hamilton, sister to my closest friend, Luke Hamilton. Along with their younger sister Grace, they've been entrusted to my care to get them safely to Oregon, where they will stay until their brother can join." His words echoed above the wind, and not a single person moved as he spoke.

"In order to keep her safe, it was decided to dress her as a boy to avoid drawing any unwanted attention. However, it's become too difficult to continue the charade while on the trail." He turned his gaze onto everyone, one by one, making sure they knew he meant his next words.

"Phoebe and Grace are under my protection. I don't believe any more needs to be said. Anyone who dares to cross the line and treat them with anything other than the utmost respect will answer to me." He waited to see the nods of the people standing around.

"How do you expect a woman to manage getting a wagon across the long difficult journey ahead, all on her own?" Titus Cain was leaning against his wagon, arms crossed in front of him.

"She needs a man to help her." He looked her up and down and the smile on his face made her uneasy.

Colton walked over to stand directly in front of the other man.

"Same way hundreds of other women have done it after they lost their husbands, fathers, and brothers along the way." His voice left no doubt that he was warning Titus to stay away from the women.

Titus pushed himself away from the wagon,

shrugged his shoulders, tipping his hat in her direction. "Well, if you ever need a hand little lady, you know where to find me."

With that, he walked away to finish checking on his own wagon.

Phoebe saw the tension in Colton's face as he watched the other man leave.

Somehow, she knew Titus Cain was going to cause trouble.

Turning to face her sister, she saw the worried look on her face. Giving her the biggest grin she could muster, she walked over and took her sister's hand. "Come on peanut...time to get back on the trail!"

No matter what, she wouldn't let her sister see how worried she was too.

CHAPTER 6

The rest of the day was difficult traveling. The mud from the rain dragged on the wheels and the wind hadn't let up for the remainder of the afternoon.

But now that they were almost to the spot where they would make camp for the night, Phoebe realized the sun was peeking through the clouds and the wind was no more than a slight breeze.

Her hands hurt from gripping the reins and tugging to control the animals that were hauling the wagon. They had been spooked for most of the day and the muddy ruts on the ground they trudged through while pulling the heavy wagon behind them weren't helping their temperament.

She watched as Colton rode toward her wagon. She couldn't help noticing how he waved and spoke with the people he passed along the way. It was obvious everyone had the highest respect for him, and he smiled and joked easily with them.

Until he saw her.

For some reason, he seemed to just stop smiling and look at her without expression. He continued toward her wagon, his eyes on her the whole time.

Why did she annoy him so much?

"We'll stop here for the night. Let the animals have some rest and the folks in the wagons can make any repairs they need to. Bring your wagon up close to the O'Hara and Thomsen wagons. Try to listen to the men in the groups and don't cause any trouble." With that, he moved past her, without ever smiling.

Phoebe scowled at his back as he rode away. "Foul tempered oaf." She couldn't help muttering her thoughts under her breath.

James and Susan O'Hara were the kindest couple she'd ever met. She felt bad about lying to them from the beginning when they had always been so kind to "Pete" and his little sister. She worried how they would act toward her when she saw them again.

She wasn't going to have to wait long to find out.

James had already arranged his wagon into the circle formation and was walking in her direction. Phoebe could see Susan bustling behind him to keep up. As she pulled her wagon to a stop beside them, Susan was waving with one hand while trying to hold her skirt up with the other.

"Oh my goodness, Phoebe! What a day you've had! You and your sister can just rest up while my James sets your animals out for the night." As she got down from the wagon, Susan grabbed her arm, then turned and clutched Grace's too. "I will have a wonderful stew made up for the whole lot of us in just a bit. You girls come sit down over here and don't you worry about a thing."

Phoebe didn't have a chance to say a word and as she glanced at her sister, their eyes met. They both struggled to hold back their laughter but they couldn't stop the smiles from reaching their lips.

They hadn't had anyone care for them like this since their own mother died, and while they knew they really should be helping the others, they couldn't resist letting the older woman dote on them, just a bit.

"We can take care of our animals and you don't need to worry about making us a meal. We can do that ourselves." Phoebe said the words half-heartedly, hoping the woman wouldn't change her mind. The thought of hot stew, and someone fussing over them, truly made her feel like a weight was lifted from her shoulders after a tiring day.

"Don't be silly! Mr. Wallace will be joining us, as well as the Thomsen's. I feel a celebration is in order after getting through that storm and to enjoy the fact that you can stop having to pretend you are a young man. It was as clear as the eyes on my face you were just a wee girl!"

Susan O'Hara had a knack for making a person feel welcome.

"You knew I was a girl?" Phoebe was surprised. In order to keep her secret, she hadn't mingled much with the others but she'd spoken to the O'Hara's on occasion. She never knew they suspected anything.

"Dear child, your eyes gave you away the first time I saw you. I knew you must have had your reasons for hiding yourself as a boy, so I never told a soul besides my James. He kept his eye on you each day, as much as he could, to make sure you didn't need any help." The woman gave a small chuckle as she placed her hand on Phoebe's arm. "He told me just the other night he thought you were more capable out here than many of the men."

Phoebe smiled at the compliment and enjoyed knowing the older man had been watching out for her. It made her heart ache for her father.

"Now, you both sit down and rest." With that, she turned and started pulling her pots out of the box on her wagon. The woman bustled around, busying herself preparing the meal. Phoebe undid her bonnet and ran her fingers through her hair. It felt so good to let her hair down. She swept it to the side and started braiding it.

A young woman with dark hair stepped out from the wagon beside them. When she turned to face Phoebe, she smiled warmly and waved.

She came closer and put her hand out to Phoebe's. "Hello, my name is Audrey Thomsen. You don't know how happy I am to discover there's another young woman making this trek across the country! I thought I was doomed to spend the entire journey listening to men patting each other on the backs over how strong and smart they are, or worse, having to make friends with Margaret MacGregor who seems to only be interested in getting herself a husband before we reach the end of this trail."

The young woman was stunningly beautiful, the kind of beautiful Phoebe had always wanted to be. But instead, she was blessed with her mother's Irish blood, bright red hair, skin as white as snow, and a tall lankiness that didn't usually draw men's admiring gazes.

Audrey Thomsen was blessed with a nice olive complexion that had been nicely tanned while on the trail and her dark hair shone in the slowly setting sunlight. The only thing she had in common with the other woman was a set of bright blue eyes. Phoebe looked into the smiling eyes peering back at her and, somehow, knew she'd found a friend.

"I am happy to meet you, too. This is my sister, Grace." She smiled at her sister who was still sitting on the crate by the wagon. "I'm sorry for not introducing myself earlier but...well, you know." She was embarrassed by the deception she'd used for the first few days of the journey.

"Oh, don't worry about that at all. I would have done the very same thing, so don't feel bad about it. We women have to do what we can to protect ourselves." A young man walked up behind Audrey as they talked.

"This is my husband, Pete. We were wed just two days before we departed Missouri." She smiled at her husband who leaned down and kissed her.

"We are heading out west to have a new start together. I have known Audrey my whole life and knew from the time we were eight years old that I would be marrying this gal." Pete continued the story while Audrey blushed.

The evening chill started to settle on the camp but the people sitting around the small fire talking and visiting didn't seem to notice.

Colton walked up just as Susan announced that the food was ready. The older woman seemed to enjoy having people to look after. And, if the smell coming from the pot over the fire was any indication, they were all about to have the best meal they'd eaten since leaving Missouri.

Phoebe noticed Colton's eyes fall on her and his usual frown creased his brow.

Deciding not to let him ruin her evening, she

put the biggest smile she could on her face. They all dished up their meals and sat down to eat.

After they finished, the men went to make sure everything was ready for the night ahead while the women cleaned up the camp and got to know each other. More people from wagons close by soon joined and the rest of the evening was spent laughing and dancing. Fiddles were brought out of wagon boxes, and voices joined together, filling the night with beautiful sounds.

Even Colton seemed to be enjoying himself and Phoebe couldn't resist pulling him up to dance. Others soon joined in or clapped along with the music.

As Colton spun her around to the song, she let herself imagine, for just a moment, that this was her life. No running from anyone. No responsibility for anyone else's safety. No promises she had to keep. No long days trekking across the country in a wagon.

She pretended she was a woman with a home and a man who cared about her.

When the song finished, they were all laughing and spirits were high.

Just when she thought nothing could spoil her evening, she noticed Titus Cain leaning against her wagon. His eyes were locked on her and, as she walked back to rest beside the others, he moved toward her.

Colton must have noticed at the same time she did because she suddenly felt his arm tense under her hand as he led her to the crates around the fire.

"Well, Miss Hamilton. You look like you are enjoying yourself." He put his hand out and bowed gallantly in front of her. "Would you do me the honor of joining me for a dance?"

She knew she couldn't say no without causing a scene. Her skin crawled as she placed her hand on his arm. Colton didn't let go of her other hand, tucked into the crook of his arm, and she thought she was going to be pulled in two directions.

"The lady is tired, Titus. She should sit down and rest." She felt Colton's apprehension.

"Oh, but she appears to be having such fun. I just hoped to share in some of that excitement with her." Titus was glaring at Colton. "Unless there is some reason it wouldn't be allowed."

He was always questioning and pushing Colton's authority as leader of the wagon train. She couldn't make out why he'd even agreed to come along if he wasn't prepared to follow the man who'd been elected to head up the wagons.

"It's fine Colton. I'm not too tired." She really didn't want to cause a spectacle when everyone was having such a good time. They all deserved a much earned relaxing evening, and she didn't want to spoil it.

"Yes, Colton. The lady can speak for herself. I promise to be on my best behavior."

She tried to offer Colton a smile to let him know she was fine but his eyes were shooting fire at Titus. He let go of her hand and she let the other man lead her out to the center where others were still laughing and dancing around, oblivious to the display between the two men.

As soon as Titus's eyes met hers, she felt her stomach knot. She missed the happiness she'd enjoyed while dancing with Colton.

He seemed determined to use her to get under Colton's skin. She realized she was going to have to be very careful when this man was around.

CHAPTER 7

Colton saw the outline of Chimney Rock on the horizon. He glanced around at the countryside, letting himself relax in the saddle and enjoy the view. The dust from the wagons behind him hadn't caught up yet, so he could take some time to breathe in the fresh air.

The day was warm and, so far, their journey had been without major incident. However, he knew people were getting tired, animals were starting to wear out, and the more days they spent on the trail, the more chances there were for things to go wrong.

He kicked his heels into his horse's sides, letting the animal race across the open ground ahead of them. He had to clear his head and he knew sitting on the back of his trusted mare, moving across the prairies, was always the answer.

He couldn't figure out why he felt the way he did around Phoebe. It hadn't been so bad when she was dressed in men's clothing but since she now dressed in her own clothes, and wore her hair loose, he had to admit something stirred in him around her.

It didn't make sense to him.

He'd been in love once or, at least at the time, he'd thought he was but he knew it wasn't *that*. There was just something about her that made him downright ornery when she was near. And, if he were honest, it wasn't always her fault.

She was a lot like his twin sister Ella, who he hadn't seen in months. Maybe that was it. Maybe he felt protective of her because of that or because of his friendship with Luke.

No matter how much he tried to convince himself that's all it was even he knew there was likely more to it than that.

But he wasn't prepared to deal with what it might mean. He'd let himself care for a woman before and he knew how much damage that could do to a man's heart.

"Colton! We need you to come back to the wagons. Pete Thomsen has taken ill. The others are helping Mrs. Thomsen to keep the wagons going but he's had to lay himself down." Colton's heart dropped. He knew he'd been too lucky so far.

He nodded to the guide who'd ridden up with

the news and whipped his horse around to head back to the wagons. Taking ill while on the trail usually didn't end well. He just hoped that Pete Thomsen was strong enough to fight whatever was ailing him.

"Tell the others to spread out and stop for a bit to see what's going on. We'll have an early afternoon meal." He knew stopping a wagon train was dangerous especially when they had to keep good time to make it through the mountains before the cold weather set in.

But he wasn't the kind of man who could force a man to keep moving if he was dangerously ill. They were making good time so far, so a bit of a rest wouldn't hurt. They could eat now instead of further up the trail.

As he neared the wagons, he could see Phoebe standing holding Audrey in her arms. The smaller woman was crying and he could tell it was all Phoebe could do to hold her up.

He pulled up beside them, then jumped down from his horse before it had even stopped moving. He looked to Phoebe and he noticed the tears in her own eyes. She simply shook her head at him, her expression grim.

He swore under his breath.

He was too late. Pete Thomsen was already gone.

✦❀✦

Phoebe leaned back against the wheel of the wagon, letting the dark envelope her. She let her tears fall, finally alone, away from the horrible sorrow the day had brought.

Everyone had finally settled in their wagons, sleeping so they could be back on the trail early the next morning. Sleep wasn't coming for her, so she'd crawled past her sister, out of the wagon, to sit under the stars, enjoying the brightness of the full moon illuminating the land with a glow as far as she could see.

She wrapped her blanket closer around her shoulders as she closed her eyes against the tears. The memories of her own mother dying from cholera ripped at her heart. It had been the same for her ma as it had been for Pete.

Both had felt fine in the morning but, within just a few hours, they were barely clinging to life.

She hoped Audrey was resting and able to get a break from her grief. Phoebe had been through the same sorrow when her mother had passed and she couldn't imagine having to deal with the pain her friend would face in the morning.

The men had buried Pete that afternoon while Phoebe stood strong beside his wailing widow, holding her shoulders and letting her friend lean on her for strength.

But they had to keep moving which meant there'd be no time to stay, getting back on the trail tomorrow. They should have continued traveling today but Phoebe knew Colton understood the grief Audrey was suffering, so had let the others vote on whether to stop early or continue.

The others agreed that, since the wagons were making good time, a few hours' extra rest wouldn't hurt.

Everyone except Titus Cain. He'd been adamant that it was foolish to stay after the man was buried. He had reminded them that it wouldn't be the last time they would lay someone to rest before reaching Oregon and they wouldn't be able to stop every time it happened.

She'd noticed Colton clenching his fists as he had walked to the man, telling him the others had voted to stop for a rest and that was the end of the discussion. Titus had glared angrily then stormed off to his own wagon.

Suddenly, Phoebe's eyes flew open. She sensed someone, or something, was watching her and she realized too late how foolish it had been to come out on her own. Not only were there strange wild animals roaming all around, she had Titus to consider as well.

"You really should be more careful. You don't know what is out here in the dark." Colton's voice startled her but realizing it was him helped get her racing heart back under control.

He came out from the shadows of the wagon just past hers. There was just enough light from the moon to see his face beneath the brim of his hat. He walked over and stood in front of her.

"I'm sorry. I couldn't sleep and I worried my tossing would keep Grace awake. The wagon creaks and moves every time I turn over." She leaned her head back on the wagon wheel, lifting her eyes up to the sky. "I needed to get some air and try to get my thoughts together."

Colton moved and folded his legs, sitting down beside her on the ground.

He leaned back and she noticed him look up at the sky, too.

They sat there in silence for what seemed like hours before he finally spoke. "How's Audrey doing?" He sounded tired.

"I'm sure she finally fell asleep from sheer grief. I worry how she will manage in the morning when we pull out again. Leaving her beloved Pete behind will surely take its toll on her."

Colton rested his elbows on his bent knees, feet flat on the ground. He bent his head forward and ran his fingers through his hair, then rested his head on his hands. As he did, his hat pushed back on his head, almost falling off.

"I had foolishly hoped we could make the trip

without any loss. I fear this won't be the last and it kills me to know I can't get everyone safely to the end of the trail." She realized just how much burden he carried with his obligation for the people who had signed on with the outfit.

"Everyone knew the dangers of the trail when they signed on, Colton. You can't shoulder the responsibility for everyone. We all signed the contracts before we left Missouri. There are some things you can't control and Pete's death was an unfortunate circumstance."

They sat quietly for a few more moments. They heard wolves howling in the distance and at the sound, the camp animals stomped and snorted uneasily.

Colton picked up a small stone and tossed it in front of him.

Phoebe looked at him, determined to change the subject and lighten his mood. "How did you and my brother meet? I know he'd gone out west to look for gold after he and my pa had a fight but I never really knew what he was doing while he was gone." She tucked her knees up under her blanket, resting her head on them.

"Then, when pa died and he came home, he was upset and didn't want to talk about much. I didn't really get to spend time with him before we were packed up and headed out to meet up with you."

Colton sat, just staring at another rock he held

in his hands, and Phoebe wondered if he would answer.

"We met up out west. We were both searching for gold, looking for something to turn our fates around. I guess we were both running from something, searching for that one thing that would bring us happiness. We thought that thing was gold." He tossed the second rock and it landed a few feet in front of him.

"We both found some gold but realized we were still searching for something, so we left, going from place to place, searching for what we felt we were missing." He shrugged his shoulders.

"Eventually, he realized what he needed was his family, so he headed back east for home. I went along with him and when we arrived, I heard there was a wagon train hiring on scouts and looking for someone to lead them to Oregon." He turned and watched her. "We went our separate ways. He was heading home to his family and I thought I may as well make myself useful while I keep searching for what it is I'm looking for."

"Where's your family Colton? Surely you must miss them too." Phoebe couldn't imagine ever being separated from her family without good reason. When her parents were alive, she would never have left them, unlike Luke. It tore her ma up terrible when he had left and Phoebe knew it had hurt her pa, too.

Colton took his hat from his head and twisted it in his hands. "My family's in Oregon. That's why your brother asked me to make sure you got there if he didn't catch up along the way. Figured my family could take you in until he made it."

"Well, that's wonderful, Colton. You will be able to see them again soon." She was happy for him to have something to look forward to. "Do you have a large family?"

He chuckled. "Could say that. Along with my ma, I have an older brother, a twin sister, and two younger brothers." He sat quietly for a moment. "My pa died on the way out to Oregon, when we traveled this trail to settle our claim many years back."

Phoebe reached out and placed her hand on his arm. "Oh Colton, I'm so sorry about your pa."

He shrugged his shoulders. "Was a long time ago."

She sensed that he didn't want to talk about it. "So, the rest of your family sounds wonderful. You must be excited to see them."

"I won't be stopping. I'll drop you and your sister off, if Luke hasn't caught us up by then, but I won't be staying." She was startled by his sharp response.

"Why? Surely it's been a while since you've seen them."

He pushed himself away from the wagon and

stood up. He slapped his hat back on his head and stared past the wagons, into the distance. Phoebe rose up too, wrapping herself tightly in her blanket.

He turned and his gaze caught hers. The quiet of the night closed in around them and Phoebe felt rooted to the spot. He reached over and lifted a dangling curl from her shoulder. He rubbed it between his fingers, then dropped it like it burned him.

"You really should get yourself back inside. We have an early start in the morning and Audrey will need you to lend a shoulder when it's time to leave."

With those words, he turned on his heels and walked away until she couldn't see him in the darkness.

Realizing she was still holding her breath, she let it go, bringing her fingers up to touch the hair he'd just held.

Unsure what had just happened or what she'd said to upset him, she leaned against the wagon for balance. Perhaps the emotions of the day had finally caught up to her.

Whatever it was, she knew Colton was right. Tomorrow would be a difficult day and she needed to keep her mind on helping her new friend deal with the heartache of leaving her husband buried on the trail behind her.

She didn't have time to figure out why Colton's proximity had weakened her knees or why he'd stared into her eyes like he wanted to say more. After seeing the pain Audrey was enduring, she knew she would never allow herself to care for someone that much.

Not when she knew how easy it was to lose someone you loved.

CHAPTER 8

"We'll rest here for a few days. Take stock of what you need and I will escort you and Grace into Fort Laramie to get your supplies. The prices here are steep and they'll take advantage of women on their own. I'm riding to the fort in about an hour, so be ready by then."

They had set up just outside of Fort Laramie last evening, later in the day than he'd hoped. After a quick evening meal, everyone went to bed knowing they would have a few days of rest to restock and make any necessary repairs to their wagons.

The travelers were exhausted; weeks on the trail caused many to question whether the journey was worth it. Losing Pete Thomsen to cholera had scared the others and they knew only too well there would be more loss along the way.

Arriving at Fort Laramie gave them all a much-needed boost, knowing they had some time to relax a bit before continuing.

"We'll be ready. Grace and I are just hanging out some of our clothing to dry. We gave them a quick wash in the creek this morning." He noticed she wasn't meeting his gaze.

He'd avoided her since the night outside her wagon. Except for the odd order here and there and to check in on them, he'd spent most of his time away from her, even taking his meals with other families in the company.

He'd come dangerously close to losing control of his emotions that night. After the day of laying Pete to rest in a makeshift grave on the side of the trail, sleep wouldn't come for him. He'd gone outside to walk around and check the camp and he saw her sitting beside the wagon with her head back, face turned to the sky.

The moon gave off enough light for him to see the tears rolling down her cheeks. He knew how much her friend's pain had affected her. During the small service and burial, Phoebe was glued to Audrey's side.

Seeing Phoebe so upset that night by her wagon had torn at his heart. He didn't want to care too much but, if he was honest, he was drawn to her more than he wanted to admit. He'd been unable to stay away, his feet carried him to her to offer her comfort.

When he'd gazed into her eyes, he found his hand reaching to touch her hair and he knew he had to get away from her.

He knew what women could do to your heart.

The truth was, he couldn't figure Phoebe out. He hadn't known many women as strong as her—besides his ma and Ella, his twin sister. Phoebe had managed to keep up with the wagon train, caring for her team of animals while also looking after her younger sister.

She hadn't complained once about some of the demands they had faced so far even when some of the men in the outfit were known to grumble about the conditions from time to time.

He still didn't understand what those girls were running from but he knew that for Luke to send his sisters on a journey like this, there had to be a good reason. What he couldn't figure out was how Luke convinced Phoebe to go along with it. After their first meeting, it was clear this was not her plan and she wasn't happy with it.

But she'd done it anyway and since getting to know her the past few weeks, he was surprised she had ever agreed to something she didn't want to do.

She was laying clothes out along the side of her wagon, still trying to avoid eye contact. He smiled and he noticed that her cheeks flushed. Obviously, he wasn't the only one affected.

"I'm going to talk to Audrey and see if she's

made her decision. If she chooses to continue on, she will likely need some more supplies, too. But if she is going to turn back, this is when she needs to decide. There will be other outfits making their way back as other emigrants change their minds and head back east. She could join on with them."

She stopped fussing with her clothes and finally looked at him. "I spoke with her last night when we arrived and she says she is still determined to follow through on the dream her and Pete had for a new life out west. She feels she owes it to him to try."

That wasn't the answer Colton had hoped to hear. Having to watch out for two young women on the trail was bad enough but having a single widow was going to give him more to worry about.

"Oh, Mr. Wallace! Thank goodness we found you!" The sound of Harriet MacGregor's voice caused him to inwardly cringe. He turned and saw the short woman scurrying toward him with her daughter right behind her.

The daughter, Margaret, was stunningly beautiful. She had yellow-blonde hair the color of fresh butter. Her skin was flawless and she was always the proper lady. Even during the long, hard days on the trail, her clothes looked perfect and her milky white complexion remained. She was a petite girl and reminded him of a delicate child in need of protection.

He glanced over at Phoebe who was also

watching the women approach. He couldn't help but compare the bright red hair that always seemed to escape from under her bonnet and skin that displayed a fair amount of freckles along her nose and cheeks, when it wasn't red from sunburn. Phoebe wasn't petite, in fact, she stood almost as tall as him.

Her clothes were dusty and wrinkled and as she stood watching the other women come toward them, she offered them a smile that he noticed didn't quite reach her eyes. As he watched, she tried smoothing her skirts and tucking her hair back under her bonnet.

"Mr. Wallace. May I please have a word?" Harriet was huffing as she reached out to put one hand on his arm and the other on her heaving chest.

"My dear Margaret needs a new bonnet and Miles left for the Fort before we woke up. Would it be too much trouble for you to take her along with you when you go? I heard you telling one of the scouts that you'd be escorting the Hamilton women there, so I hoped one more wouldn't cause you any extra hardship."

Margaret stood there looking down demurely at her feet before peeking up at Colton from under the perfectly fine bonnet she was already wearing on her head. She gave him a shy smile but something in her eyes made him wonder how much of that was for her mother's benefit.

"I'm sorry, Harriet, but I'll already have my hands full helping the Hamilton ladies, as well as Audrey Thomsen, restock their supplies. We'll be here for a couple of days, so you will have plenty of time to make your way to the fort with your husband before we leave."

Margaret appeared close to tears. Her bottom lip started quivering. "But I don't want to wait! I've had to wear this same bonnet for weeks now and it's a horrible mess! Please Mr. Wallace, I promise I won't be any trouble!" She placed her small hand on his arm, batting her eyelashes for good measure.

He sensed Phoebe walk up beside him. He turned to look at her, hoping she would help him find a way out of this.

"Margaret, Mr. Wallace will bring you along with us. My sister and I can look after ourselves quite well without him watching over us every second and my friend, Audrey, will stay with us. One more woman along won't be too much trouble at all."

He was sure he'd never seen a bigger smile on her face. She had witnessed the incessant hounding Harriet MacGregor made of Colton with her daughter; in fact, the entire wagon train had seen the constant harassment. It was a bit of a running joke among the travelers.

Harriet was determined to have her daughter married to Colton before the end of the trail. He knew she'd heard the rumors about his gold strike in

California and he had no doubt that had planted the thought of marriage in her head. It didn't matter if it was true or not, in her mind, she wasn't taking any chances.

And for what it was worth, Margaret didn't seem to have her own opinion, either way.

He shot Phoebe a look, letting her know he didn't appreciate her assistance. She turned up her smile even more; he was almost certain she was struggling to hold back laughter.

There was no way he could refuse to take Margaret without looking like a heel.

Keeping his gaze on Phoebe, he decided he wouldn't let her win that easily.

"Of course we can take her along with us. I'll ride ahead with my horse and Margaret is welcome to ride in the wagon with Phoebe." He smiled at Phoebe, enjoying her expression when she realized she'd be stuck listening to the other woman during the trip to the fort.

"I will be back in an hour. She can stay here with Phoebe until I can get back to take them. I'm sure she'd love the company!"

He almost whistled as he walked away. The look on Phoebe's face gave him the first genuine smile he had in days.

CHAPTER 9

P hoebe cringed as Margaret's voice carried to
her ears. The other woman was riding in the
back of the wagon, complaining that the sun was
too hot to be out in, even for the short trip to the
fort. Grace and Audrey walked beside the wagon
and she scowled at Colton's back as he rode ahead
of them on his horse.

They'd spent a few hours walking around the
fort, picking up needed supplies. She had hoped to
have the chance to speak privately with Audrey but
Margaret made that impossible.

"I still can't believe you spoke to those heathens!
I thought for sure they'd be throwing you on the
back of their horses and riding off with you! You
really must be more careful out here!"

They'd met up with two Indian women and
some of their men mounted on massive horses as

they were leaving the fort. The natives approached the wagon cautiously and Phoebe noticed Colton quickly make his way to them.

Phoebe had stopped the wagon and walked over to offer greetings, with the sound of Margaret's wailing in the back of the wagon piercing her ears. One of the native women had held a beautiful, beaded necklace in her hands. The necklace was made with the brightest blue stones she'd ever seen, woven onto leather straps. It was truly stunning.

Phoebe had watched as the woman held it out toward Grace, placing it against her golden hair. It seemed like it was made for her.

Knowing they didn't have any money to spare on trinkets, her heart sank when Grace's eyes lit up for the first time in months. Grace had held the necklace in her hand, running her fingers over the beautiful beadwork, admiring the piece of jewelry unlike anything they'd ever seen before.

The woman had smiled at Phoebe, then reached up and touched her bonnet, the one her ma had made for her to wear for special occasions. She'd dug it out of her trunk knowing she would finally be seeing a bit of civilization today.

The woman had nodded toward her bonnet, still touching the soft material.

Phoebe had removed it from her head and handed it to the woman, watching as Grace realized she was trading it for the necklace. Grace had grabbed for the bonnet, telling her not to do it, but Phoebe desperately wanted to see the smile stay on her sister's face, so she'd shushed her as the other woman tied the necklace around her neck.

Now, as they made their way back, Phoebe turned her head to her sister as she walked beside the wagon. Grace was still touching the beads and lifting them up to admire them.

She would've traded everything she had to see that happiness on her sister's face.

Margaret continued whining from the back. "And then to trade your good bonnet. Now all you'll have is that dirty, worn out, old, ripped one you wear every day. I would never trade something as nice as that!"

Phoebe smiled to herself. Of course she wouldn't. Margaret likely had ten beautiful bonnets tucked away in her trunks and had just picked up a nice new yellow one today at the fort. Phoebe would have loved to have a new bonnet to wear but she had to be careful of what they spent on their way to Oregon.

Obviously, Margaret didn't have the same worry.

"Margaret, those women weren't threatening at all. Colton wouldn't have let us speak to them if they were going to cause trouble." She was glad they were almost back to camp. Spending the day listening to Margaret had tired her out. Colton hadn't been much help and had insisted on getting the supplies they all needed, while the women looked around and helped Margaret.

She was regretting her haste this morning while enjoying Colton's discomfort.

"And, Grace has been through a rough time and deserved something nice. She's still a young girl and I wanted to make her happy." She didn't think Margaret would understand but she told her anyway.

The wagon hit a rut, jostling it to the side, then it banged back down hard on the other side. She had a hard time not laughing out loud at the thump she heard in the back. "For goodness sakes, Phoebe! Be more careful! I am being thrown around back here like a sack of flour."

"Terribly sorry, Margaret, I didn't see the rut." The smirk on her face said otherwise and she realized that Colton had come up right beside her as they arrived at camp. He had heard the exchange. One eyebrow went up as he tried his best not to smile too.

He'd been quite pleasant that day and Phoebe realized he wasn't always so ornery. She assumed he had to be stricter since he was the trail boss while the wagons were moving but when they were resting, he could afford to be a little more agreeable.

Bringing her wagon back into camp, right beside Audrey's and the O'Hara's, Phoebe reached up to smooth her hair. Not having a bonnet for the ride back to camp made her hair a bit of a mess. Grace was already excitedly showing Susan O'Hara the new necklace around her neck and Phoebe smiled as the older woman made a big fuss over it.

"Mr. Wallace, could I please have your assistance? I'm positively exhausted after the trip to the fort and would like to get back to my own wagon to get freshened up." Margaret's voice cut through her thoughts. Colton had tied his horse to the back of the Thomsen wagon and had been about to help Phoebe down from her seat.

Phoebe shrugged her shoulders and smiled down at him. "Better hurry and help Margaret. She's had a very trying day."

"Margaret can wait." He held his hand up for hers. His eyes held hers, almost daring her to refuse him.

She stood and took his hand, putting a foot onto the small step at the side of the wagon. Before she turned to grab the side of the wagon, Colton lifted her down to stand in front of him. She gasped and put her hands on his arms for balance.

He smiled down at her shocked expression, then slowly let her go. He tipped his hat, then turned to help Margaret out of the back of the wagon.

Smoothing out her skirt, Phoebe glanced around to see if anyone else had noticed. Audrey was smiling in her direction, so she gave a quick wave then turned to unhitch the oxen so she could start preparing their evening meal.

She needed a minute to compose herself. Surely it was just the sun beating down on her uncovered head that was causing her to feel so flushed.

"I do hope you can come and join us for supper this evening, Mr. Wallace, as a thank you for taking me to the fort." Margaret tucked her hair in around her new bonnet and Phoebe felt a momentary pang of jealousy at how beautiful the woman looked.

Averting her eyes, she pretended not to hear them talking and kept working to undo the team. Her hands trembled though, causing her to fumble.

"Well, that's awful nice of you Margaret but, truth is, it was Phoebe who was kind enough to take you to the fort. I simply provided an escort." She peeked up between the heads of the oxen and caught him looking directly at her.

"Besides, I already promised Phoebe and Grace I would eat with them tonight." He gave her a stern look leaving no doubt she wasn't supposed to argue otherwise. She put her head down and got back to work before he could see her grin.

Struggling with the harness on the last ox, Phoebe didn't hear him come up beside her. When his hand suddenly appeared and reached out to undo the harness with ease she jumped. His hand brushed against hers as he lifted off the yoke.

"Thanks for not giving me away. I just didn't

think I could spend another minute, never mind an entire evening, with that woman. I'd rather eat alone than listen to her endless prattling." He held the reins and she stepped aside as he led the oxen out to graze with the other animals.

"Well, you're more than welcome to join us for our meal. I have a great deal to discuss with Audrey about the journey ahead and it would likely be a good idea for you to be there, anyway."

She didn't want to admit she actually looked forward to his company.

He nodded. "I appreciate the invite. I'll be back once I get a chance to clean up a bit and check on everyone."

She watched him walk away, wondering why her heart was racing. The sun must have really done a number on her.

CHAPTER 10

The sun beat down on the traveling wagons, wearing on the patience of the people making their way across the open land. Phoebe walked beside the wagon, taking a break from the jostling of the rig while Audrey handled the driving.

The first night at Fort Laramie, Phoebe had sat down with the new widow and they decided, instead of both of them dragging wagons across the prairies, they would team up. Audrey sold her wagon at the fort but they kept the oxen as spare livestock for the trip ahead.

They transferred all of Audrey's possessions to Phoebe's wagon, which wasn't a lot, since the newly-wed couple had started out without much of their own belongings.

The women decided that working together

would be much easier than trying to make the rest of the trip on their own.

Grace walked beside Phoebe and they spread out enough to pick up any buffalo chips they could find for their evening fire. Spotting one just ahead on the trail, Phoebe bent to pick it up and place it in the basket she carried.

Sweat trickled down the back of her neck as she walked through the clouds of dust hanging in the air. Her hair stuck to her neck where it hung free from her torn, old bonnet.

"How much longer do you think it will take before Luke catches up with us, Phoebe? Do you think he'll ever find us?" Grace peered at her with big blue eyes full of questions.

"Of course he will, Grace. It's Luke—he wouldn't give up until he found us." She bent to grab another buffalo chip. "I'm sure he will catch up to us before we even get to Oregon."

They walked in silence for a few moments but Phoebe could tell by the crease in her sister's brow that she had more questions.

"I wonder if he was able to prove anything about Uncle Ivan." Grace shuddered. "I sure hope we never have to go back."

"Even if Luke doesn't find anything, or catch up to us right away, we won't go anywhere near that man ever again Grace. That's a promise."

Phoebe tried to put the memory of finding her

uncle pushing himself against her sister out of her mind. The stench of alcohol on his breath had overpowered her the minute she walked in the room. Her sister was crying, begging him to let her go, but he kept bringing his mouth down to hers, drowning out her cries for help.

Without thinking of the consequences, Phoebe had grabbed the rifle from the case by the door and cocked it loud enough to get through his drunken stupor.

"Let her go and get away from her. Now." She had leveled it at him as he stumbled to turn around and face her.

She could still remember the sneer on his face as he finally focused enough to see her. "And what'er ya gonna do with that? Yer a no good for nothing girl who can't even do the simple chores I ask of 'er to help pay for lookin' after the lot of ya." He was slurring as he spoke, weaving back and forth, trying to keep his balance.

He had wobbled toward her. "I'm jus' takin' some payment for what's owed me... Gracey here's a lovely young girl and it'd do you both well to remember how I've taken ye both in since yer parents are gone. Without me, you'd both be on the streets."

"Keep your hands off Grace. You haven't done anything to help us. I take care of everything around here for you and you have the money from the settlement for the mercantile fire. Money that was supposed to be for me and Grace."

He'd lunged toward her, falling against a stool instead. He banged his head as he fell, knocking himself out long enough for Phoebe and Grace to get safely to another room. By morning, they were assured he wouldn't remember a thing... He never did.

But the events of that evening left no doubt in Phoebe's mind that she had to get Grace away from their uncle. Phoebe knew she was safe from her uncle's advances because he'd made no secret of his distaste for her bright red hair, tall lanky body, or her attitude. He liked Grace who was blonde, small, and quiet.

That's why she packed up everything they had and prepared to leave as soon as she could find where her uncle hid the money. She wasn't going to stay there and let him hurt her sister.

Not after the promise she'd made to her ma, just before she died. Her ma was worried about Grace and asked Phoebe to always look out for her. Phoebe had promised she would.

Luckily for them, Luke had shown up a few days later. Phoebe told him everything and he'd wasted no time getting them out of there.

Now, as she walked beside her sister, Phoebe realized just how much it bothered Grace to think they might ever have to go back to St. Louis. She didn't know where their new home would be but Phoebe knew it would never be anywhere near *that* man.

⚜

THE WAGON TRAIN suffered more loss over the next few days; first, when one of the scouts was accidentally shot while hunting bison in the area.

The following day, a mother and her young child succumbed to the fever, leaving the entire outfit mourning the lives lost.

Colton felt the strain of burying some of the people he had come to know and leaving them behind on the trail without even a marker to remember them.

He'd also seen the sorrow in Phoebe's face and he knew that each time they buried another person, it affected them all.

Despite their troubles, they were still making good time and he knew they'd make it to Independence Rock within the next few days. Once there, they could enjoy a day or two of rest before continuing. It was only the end of June, so they were ahead of schedule and could afford to take the time to rest.

Colton was tired. The constant worry over Phoebe and her sister and now Audrey wore on him. Titus Cain argued with him over every decision and seemed intent on being around Phoebe every chance he could.

Not that he was jealous; he just didn't trust the man to keep his hands to himself. And, he knew Luke was counting on him to make sure both of his sisters made the trip with their reputations intact.

He made the rounds of the wagons and doubled back to make sure everyone was getting along all right. Harriet and Margaret held him up when he went by their wagon, asking when they could stop for the evening since they were exhausted and tired of being bumped around in the wagon.

He'd repeatedly told them that walking along-side the wagon would be a lot easier on their bodies than jostling around in the back. They would walk for a while until one or the other couldn't take another step.

Harriet's bedraggled husband had made a comfortable sitting area out of quilts and cushions for them in the back. So, for most of the journey, that is where they could be found.

As the dust from the wagons settled, he noticed Phoebe standing to the side of the trail next to a pile of rocks on the ground. He glanced ahead and saw the wagons making their way along, unaware that she'd stopped.

He rode toward her just as she walked over to where some wild flowers were growing under a tree nearby. He watched as she bent down, picked a handful of flowers, and then turned back to the spot where she'd been standing.

He came up alongside her and noticed tears in her eyes.

"Are you all right, Phoebe?" Worried she was hurt or sick, he jumped down from his horse and reached for her arm.

She nodded her head to an area on the ground and he looked to see what upset her.

1843
J Hembree

Amid a pile of rocks stood one taller rock with those words carved in its surface.

"It just seems so sad, laying out here alone on a trail with no family or anyone nearby to ever stop and pay their respects. I figured it was the least I could do for someone who had traveled this trail ahead of me." She bent and laid the flowers in front of the stones.

"All of their hopes for a future out west, taken from them. Their family had to leave him behind just like Audrey had to leave Pete. And, like we've had to leave the others..." Her voice choked as she placed her hand on the grave marker.

He wasn't sure what to do, so he just placed his hand on her shoulder.

"We don't know if it was a young man, woman, old man, or worse—a child."

He crouched down beside her then reached over to push a wisp of her hair back under her bonnet. The sadness in her eyes as she lifted them tugged at his heart.

Before he knew what he was doing, he was standing and pulling her into his arms.

"You said, yourself, we all knew what we agreed to when we signed on with these wagon trains. For some, the chance to own their own land in the Oregon Territory is an opportunity they would never have anywhere else. A chance for a new life, a place of their own. There are always risks but for those who do make it, the dream will live on through them."

She was letting him hold her in his arms and he could feel her arms around his waist as she let her head rest on his chest.

He swallowed hard, knowing he should let her go or risk her reputation but holding her felt better than he was willing to admit.

He continued embracing her, not wanting the moment to end too soon. "We came out to Oregon the same year—1843. I was only about 15 years old but I was headstrong and determined to help my pa get the new land settled so we could build an empire."

He struggled for words and he looked down as Phoebe stepped back to peer up into his face.

Not wanting to look in her eyes as he continued, he let his gaze fall past her to the dust of the wagons in the distance.

"My pa drowned saving me from the Snake River before we could reach Oregon."

"Oh Colton! I'm so sorry!" She placed her hand on his chest and there were tears in her eyes. He didn't think he'd ever met a woman who cared as deeply about others as she did.

"I wouldn't listen to him, insisting I could get the animals across, but I hadn't realized the depth of the water or how strong the current was. He managed to get me back on my horse and to the edge of the river but the current was too strong."

"It wasn't your fault, Colton. You can't blame yourself."

"I've always blamed myself. And, I have no doubt my brothers, and even my sister Ella, have thought it as well."

He wasn't sure why he was telling Phoebe any of this. He'd never spoken the words out loud before. He pulled back from her, starting to feel uncomfortable.

He cleared his throat then turned and mounted his horse, holding his hand down for her to take. "We better catch up before someone notices us missing."

Phoebe turned around one last time and placed one of the flowers right on top of the tombstone. She kissed her fingers, then placed them on the rock before standing and reaching for his hand.

"Sorry, I don't have a side-saddle for a lady to ride on but if you want to sit sideways in front of me, I can hold you on that way."

Before he knew it, she had placed her foot on top of his and was jumping up behind him in the saddle.

"I'm fine like this. I've never liked riding side-saddle anyway." With that, she put her arms around his waist.

He kicked his heels into his horse's flanks and raced to catch up with the others, needing to get space between them as fast as possible before he did something he would regret.

CHAPTER 11

They had made camp late last night, arriving at Independence Rock well past dark. Colton had pushed them to continue, knowing once they made it, they would all be able to enjoy a short rest before moving on.

Phoebe was up early. She hadn't slept well the past few nights and she didn't want to keep tossing and turning in the wagon in case she woke Grace and Audrey up.

It was nice having Audrey travel with them. Sharing the wagon at night was tight, making space among the extra supplies but they made it work. They didn't have a tent or anything else to use, so they made do with what they had.

Some nights, Phoebe would lay awake listening to the sounds of the night. Coyotes and wolves howled all night and other animal noises would often join in. She could hear the snorting and moving of the livestock out grazing overnight.

Many nights, Grace would snuggle up to her sister as close as she could get, obviously afraid of the noises outside the wagon. Phoebe was just as scared but would never admit it to Grace. Now, with Audrey there too, it didn't seem as scary.

No one else was up yet, so Phoebe tried to be quiet as she got the fire going to put on some coffee, biscuits, and bacon for their breakfast. Most of the travelers would most likely sleep in as late as possible, enjoying a day of rest. Colton usually had them all on the trail by seven, so they were always up long before dawn, having breakfast then packing up for the day. Today would be a much-needed break for them all.

"You're up early. And, I'm surprised to see you don't have your guardian stuck to your skirts like he normally is." Titus Cain came around the side of the wagon, surprising Phoebe.

"Oh, Titus, you startled me! I thought I was the only one awake." Her hand flew up to her chest, almost causing her to drop the pot she was trying to hang above the fire. Titus reached out and took it from her before it fell, then hung it on the hook for her.

"Sorry, didn't mean to frighten you. I was just out checking on the animals. I thought I heard a noise but it must have just been you."

He didn't seem as ornery as he usually was. He was, actually, a nice looking man, when he wasn't scowling. His hair was a nice color of brown and his eyes were a striking hazel color. She hadn't noticed before because he always seemed so angry and ready to argue about everything.

"So, how do you know Colton Wallace so well?" He certainly wasn't subtle. If he wanted to find something out, he just came out with it. "I assume you must have known him for a while since he's always hanging around you and your sister."

She wasn't sure what he was getting at or why he thought it was any of his business.

"Colton is my brother, Luke's, friend. He asked Colton to look after us until he could join us." She didn't think he needed to know any more than that. But, apparently, he still had questions.

He sat down on a crate by the wagon and leaned back with his legs stretched out in front of him. "Seems to me he has more of an interest than just looking after his friend's younger sisters." Titus was watching her intently.

She could feel her cheeks heat up when she real-ized what he was insinuating.

"Funny how he always seems to be hanging around you. And, he won't even let anyone else talk to you. This is the first time since we've been on the trail that I've been able to get you alone long enough to speak to you and express my interest in perhaps getting to know you better myself. I might just be looking to settle down myself when I get to the end of the trail."

"Well, I'm flattered Titus but I'm just not sure what we will be doing when my brother joins us. I need to consider my sister and getting her to Oregon. I don't have the time to be thinking of much else." Phoebe didn't know how to let him know she wasn't interested in pursuing anything more.

His lip curled up in a sneer. "You think you're too good for someone like me? I may not have a lot of money but once I'm finished taking care of some business in Oregon, I plan on settling my own farm and could offer any woman a good life."

She was beginning to feel very uncomfortable, realizing his intentions. He wasn't someone who took rejection well.

"I'm a single man, and you're a single woman, alone on this trail. I can offer you protection as well as a good future. Your reputation is at risk every day you continue on this trail without a man. Especially when you have the likes of Colton Wallace sniffing around you every minute. Some of the others have already started talking."

She stopped stirring her biscuit mixture. "What do you mean people are talking? What are they saying?"

He shrugged his shoulders. "Some people are

questioning exactly who you are and why he seems so interested in you. He hasn't been as efficient as he should be in the duties he was hired on to do, spending so much time checking on and keeping his eye on you." He paused for a second to make sure he had her attention.

"Some are saying they think maybe you aren't as *wholesome* as you'd let everyone believe."

Her mouth dropped open as she realized exactly what he was saying.

He put his hands up as though to stop her from speaking. "Of course, I've defended your honor at every turn but any time Colton has been asked about the situation, he gets defensive and tells the others it's none of their concern. The men in this company just want to make sure he's doing the job he was hired to do and that he isn't getting distracted. Or, that he isn't putting your reputation in danger."

Phoebe felt bad they were questioning Colton because of her. She was shocked to realize what others were saying about her reputation. Looking down at the mixing bowl, she suddenly didn't feel very hungry.

"Good morning, Phoebe. Why didn't you wake me so I could help you with breakfast?" She was so happy to hear Audrey's voice. "Oh, good morning, Titus. I didn't see you sitting there." Phoebe almost smiled when she heard the lack of excitement in her friend's voice at seeing the other man beside the wagon. It was no secret that Audrey didn't care for him.

"Good morning, Mrs. Thomsen. I was just getting ready to go check on my animals anyway. Just saying a good morning to Phoebe." He stood up, then reached out to lay his hand on Phoebe's arm. "Just think about what I said. It isn't just you that you need to think about. You need to think about your sister too."

Phoebe watched him walk away. Maybe he wasn't all that bad. At least he was trying to defend her if the others were questioning her reputation.

"What was that all about?" Audrey came over and started placing bacon into the pan to fry.

"It was nothing. He was just letting me know he was offering his protection if I need it."

She didn't know how to tell Audrey what the others in the outfit were saying about her.

"Hmmm...yes, I'm sure he is. He's had his eye on you from the minute he found out you were a woman." Audrey reached her hand out now to stop Phoebe from stirring the biscuit batter. "I'm pretty sure that's mixed enough." She kept her hand there as she looked at Phoebe. "Be careful around him, Phoebe. I don't trust him."

Phoebe offered her friend a faint smile. "Don't worry, Audrey. I know to be careful around men like him." But she also knew that a woman alone facing a ruined reputation might not have many other options available to her. She didn't want Grace suffering because of her.

She would have to be careful not to let anyone think Colton was being anything more than a concerned wagon boss. If that meant keeping herself away from him as much as possible, she would have to do it.

But she also hated to admit how much she was going to miss being around him.

CHAPTER 12

Colton's mood matched the grey skies and the rain that poured down over him. The wind whipped hard, forcing some of the wagons to stop as the canvas was lifted, exposing the contents to the rain. The muddy road was making for difficult traveling and he knew he should make the call to stop for the day.

But his foul mood wanted to make them all suffer a bit. He knew it was irrational but he was still feeling the anger he'd held on to for days.

After being confronted by a team of men from the outfit, with Titus Cain as the leader, about his distraction caring for all of the single women on the train, he'd been angry. But, then, to have woken up early the morning after arriving at Independence Rock to see Titus sitting down and talking with Phoebe, his bad temper had only increased.

He didn't know why. It wasn't like he had a claim to Phoebe. He certainly didn't want to be tied down with a woman anyway, so he couldn't understand why he was so disgruntled.

He didn't trust Titus, so he figured maybe that's what was eating at him. When he'd agreed to take Luke's sisters along with him, he'd made the unspoken vow that he would look out for them. Having a man like Titus hanging around wasn't going to be good news for any of them.

"We can't keep pushing the animals like this. Dragging these heavy wagons through the rain like this is going to wear them out. We can't afford to lose any more animals." The scout out ahead with him caught up to voice his concerns.

They'd already lost many animals along the way. Some had died of exhaustion and hunger, some had drowned, and some had been too weak to continue so had to be put down. Worse, though, was that they'd lost four more people. Over the few days since leaving Independence Rock, an older couple had succumbed to an illness they all suspected was cholera. A man had been accidentally shot while cleaning his gun and the one that weighed heavily on Colton's shoulders was the young boy who had fallen under the wheels of the wagon he was riding on.

He could still hear the wails of the mother as they buried her son on the trail.

After the excitement of Independence Rock, it was a hard blow. Just days before, they'd been resting and celebrating arriving at the giant boulder that indicated they were ahead of schedule. Everyone had spent the day reading the names of those who'd signed the rock on their way west, then added their own names to the landmark. Kids had raced around, squealing with excitement, while having the day to just be kids.

Colton had walked to the rock with Phoebe, Grace, and Audrey but Phoebe seemed to be keeping her distance from him. He'd helped Grace carve her name while Phoebe kept their conversation to a minimum.

He was sure it had something to do with her conversation with Titus that morning but he never had the opportunity to ask her about it. The day had been spent with everyone having some much-needed fun, with music and dancing, while the families in the outfit celebrated making it this far, with hopes for the futures they were heading toward.

Whenever he went near Phoebe, she seemed on edge, trying to avoid him.

Now, days later, she was still going out of her way to be cool toward him. He noticed Titus hanging around her more and it caused him concern. But Phoebe was a grown woman and if that's the kind of man she wanted to have paying her attention, then he couldn't stop her.

Looking back at the wagons struggling through the mud, Colton decided it was time to stop.

"All right. You start telling the ones to the south to start pulling up for the day and I will go from the other end." He knew he was choosing that end because he wanted to check in on Phoebe but he didn't care. He would just make sure she was managing, then he'd move on to the next wagon.

As he was riding up to the wagons, he noticed Phoebe's was stopped already, tilting to one side. When he got closer, he noticed Audrey driving the team but he didn't see either of the other girls. He could see a wheel was stuck in the mud but all of the other wagons had already moved past them and hadn't noticed. The wagon tilted at a dangerous angle.

Audrey spotted him and stood up to wave to him.

"Colton! We are hopelessly stuck and Phoebe is in the back with Grace. She hasn't been feeling well since we left this morning and Phoebe is worried about her." Colton's heart sank.

If anything happened to Grace, he didn't know if Phoebe could handle it. Racing to the back of the wagon, he jumped off his horse straight onto the step. Pulling back the canvas, he could see Phoebe staring up at him with tears in her eyes as she held her sister's head on her lap, brushing the hair back from her forehead.

"She's not well, Colton." The fear in her voice made his stomach turn.

He knew he had to get her somewhere more comfortable and it was likely going to take the men some time to get this wagon unstuck. Until then, Grace needed to be kept warm and comfortable.

Taking his arms out of his jacket, he reached down and wrapped the young girl in its warmth. Covering her head, he whispered to her that he was going to take care of her and that everything would be all right. But his heart was heavy as he thought about what could happen.

He tried not to look at Phoebe but she grabbed his arm as he turned with Grace in his arms. "Is she going to be all right?" The words were quiet and her voice caught on a sob at the end.

He clenched his teeth. This wasn't something he had any control over but he was going to do every-thing he could to avoid losing another child on this journey. Especially not Grace.

"I'll take her to the O'Hara wagon. I will come back to get you and Audrey to take you there to care for her until we can get your wagon out of the mud."

He wasn't going to make any promises that he couldn't keep. With that, he lifted the young girl out and hopped onto the back of his horse. He held her safely in front of him as he raced toward the wagons now stopped ahead.

"Susan! Grace has taken ill and needs some-where to rest until we can get their wagon out of the mud. I will go back and get Phoebe. James, can you grab a few men and come back to the wagon and help to get it unstuck?"

The older couple moved with surprising quick-ness as they made room for Grace in the wagon. Colton laid Grace gently on the blankets they'd placed on the floor of the wagon.

"Don't you worry about a thing, sweetheart. I will take good care of you until your sister gets here." Susan was fussing over the girl but Colton suspected Grace was too scared to hear what anyone was saying. Her eyes were full of fear as she looked at Colton.

"Mr. Wallace, what's going to happen to me?" Her face was flush with fever and he knew she was thinking the worst. She'd seen others die from illness, including her own mother.

"You'll be fine, Grace. Let Mrs. O'Hara take care of you for a few minutes while I get Phoebe. We'll make sure you get all better." He offered her a weak smile, trying to keep the worry from showing on his face.

He knew that no matter how much you promise, sometimes there was nothing you could do to change the outcome. He just prayed this wasn't one of those times.

CHAPTER 13

It had been at least two hours since the wagons had stopped for the day. The wind was still tossing them around and the rain was hitting the canvas in a steady downpour. The inside of the wagon was chilly but the amount of heat coming from Grace terrified the others.

She'd brought up all of the food in her stomach and continued to heave every time she tried to drink any water. She'd been in and out of consciousness, awake just long enough to let them see how scared she was.

Phoebe tried her hardest to keep herself calm, knowing she needed to control her emotions when Grace needed her.

But it was tearing her apart. She knew too well what was likely happening and she'd never felt so helpless in her life.

No matter how hard she tried to stop it, she could feel a tear escaping.

"Phoebe, I'm thirsty." Her sister's hoarse voice broke through her grief. She was alone in the wagon with Grace, while Audrey and the O'Haras set up camp and made something to eat.

"Here, let me help you sit up..." She put her hands behind Grace's head and gently tugged to help her up enough to drink. Phoebe put the metal cup up to Grace's lips, letting the cool liquid dribble down her throat.

Her sister coughed a bit, choking on the water hitting the dryness of her throat. The one good thing about the weather was the fresh, clean water the rain was providing. She knew as soon as they'd stopped, James O'Hara and Colton had dragged a large empty barrel outside that had been emptied of flour to collect rainwater to give Grace.

"Is that better?" Desperate to hear her sister say she was feeling better, Phoebe looked longingly into her eyes to see if there was any improvement. She knew if it was cholera, it would move fast. But if they could keep her hydrated, they might have a small chance to fight it.

And, she kept telling herself, maybe it wasn't cholera at all. In truth, she'd witnessed the terrible agony and diarrhea suffered by her mother, and then those on this wagon train that had succumbed to the illness, but hadn't seen any of that with Grace.

That gave her some hope.

But Grace was very sick and they both knew it. Out here, they didn't have a doctor to care for them when they got ill. They were completely at the mercy of any sickness that came along, relying only on their own strength to fight it.

Grace took her hand. Phoebe felt the heat coming from her skin.

"Ma and pa would sure be surprised if they knew we were out here on a wagon train heading west, wouldn't they?" Grace was trying to talk about anything that would take their minds off the seriousness of what was happening.

Phoebe smiled down at her sister. "Well, they'd likely be surprised you were out here but I doubt they would be too shocked to hear I was." She stroked her sister's forehead as she held it on her lap. She was leaning against a crate sitting on the side of the O'Hara's wagon. Susan had insisted Grace not be moved again, letting them stay in their wagon.

They had pitched a tent outside in the rain, even though Phoebe had offered to let them stay in her wagon.

"What will we do when we get to Oregon? What if Luke doesn't catch up with us?" She choked on a sob. "Phoebe, what if you're all alone when you get there?" A tear rolled from her eye.

"Stop it, Grace! I won't let you think like that."

"I know you don't want to, Phoebe, but you have to think about it. What will you do?" Grace was looking at her with worry.

"Grace, I'm not letting anything happen to you. So please, stop talking like that." Phoebe was having a hard time holding herself together and hearing Grace talk like she was giving up scared her.

She bent forward to place a kiss on her sister's forehead, hoping it would distract her so she wouldn't notice the tears she had in her own eyes.

Outside, the rain finally sounded like it was stopped and they could hear the people from the wagons starting to move around. Whispered voices could be heard outside the canvas as others came to ask Audrey or the O'Hara's how Grace was doing.

"Will you marry Mr. Wallace?" Phoebe shot back up at the question asked so quietly she almost thought she'd heard it wrong.

"Why would you think that, Grace?" She didn't even know what to say.

Grace gave a weak smile. "I've seen how he looks at you. And, you look at him the same way."

Phoebe sat staring at her sister in confusion.

But before she could answer, her sister started to moan, rolling to her side to bring up the small bit of water she'd swallowed. Phoebe held her sister, crying softly to herself as she felt the muscles in her small body convulse with every retch.

With every spasm, she felt her own heart tightening with fear. Closing her eyes, she softly whispered, *"I'm sorry mama. I promise I tried."* She set her sister's head back onto her lap, grateful to see that sleep had taken hold. As she glanced down at the ashen face she loved so much, she gave in to her tears.

ॐ

THE MORNING SUN was already beating on the canvas, heating the inside to an unbearable temperature. Grace's fever was still running high and Phoebe knew the extra heat was going to make her even more uncomfortable.

Her sister wasn't any better but she also hadn't got any worse overnight, so Phoebe hoped that was a good sign. Grace was in and out of consciousness and Phoebe had managed to get a little water in her that seemed to be staying down.

She hadn't heard the call for the wagons to move yet but she knew they'd need to be going soon. Phoebe worried how her sister would handle being jostled around in a moving wagon.

Audrey opened the back flap and stepped inside. "You go and get yourself some breakfast and have a wash. We're waiting for Colton before we move out. He's gone ahead somewhere, so until he comes back, we aren't sure what the plan for today is."

Thankful for the chance to get out of the hot

wagon for a few moments, Phoebe let Audrey take her place holding Grace's head in her lap. "Thank you Audrey. I don't know what I would do without a friend like you." She was feeling very weepy today, with a lack of sleep and concern over her sister bringing her to tears easily.

Audrey just smiled and shooed her out of the wagon.

Stepping out into the sunlight, Phoebe shielded her eyes from the sudden brightness. Where yesterday had been wet, windy, and chilly, today was the opposite. The sun had dried most of the ground and the heat already indicated how hot the day was going to be.

Immediately, Susan O'Hara was over taking her arm and dragging her toward a crate by the fire. "You sit yourself down here and have some breakfast. We don't need you getting sick yourself, then you'd be no help to anyone." Pouring some coffee into a cup, she handed it to Phoebe. "Drink this up. You must be nearly exhausted."

She gave the woman a smile. Since they'd stopped yesterday, she had fussed and cared for both her and Grace, making sure they had everything they needed.

"James has gone off somewhere with Colton this morning so we're all just waiting to see what the orders will be. I sure hope we won't move out today when your sister isn't well. Being tossed around in a bumpy wagon is no way for a young girl to be treated when she is sick."

"Did Colton say what we would do?" Phoebe hoped they could stay even just one more day but she knew he would have to make the decision of what would be best for the rest of the wagons in the outfit.

They'd normally already been traveling for a few hours by now and as she looked around, she could tell the others weren't sure if they should be packing up or not. Many of them were glancing her direction with sympathy, whispering to themselves. She knew that they were all likely sure Grace wasn't getting better and waiting here wasn't going to make any difference.

Peering down into her cup to try getting a hold of the tears threatening to escape, she suddenly felt Susan's arm go around her shoulders and bring her close. The past few hours had taken a toll on her and she finally just let herself cry. The older woman stroked her hair and just let her get it all out.

"I'm so scared. I feel like I've let everyone down. I just feel so helpless." All of the feelings that had been playing in her mind came tumbling out. "Why couldn't it be me who got sick? Grace is so kind and sweet and I'm supposed to be taking care of her!"

"My dear child, you are doing everything you can. Why on earth would you ever think you are letting anyone down? Nothing that has happened has been in your control."

Phoebe sat staring at the coffee in her hands trying to compose herself before continuing. "I promised my ma. Now I've let her down."

Sitting back and holding Phoebe back to look into her eyes, Susan stared at her in shock. "What did you say, child?" Phoebe had said it so quietly the other woman hadn't heard her.

"I promised my ma. When she was so sick, I went in to see her. She was in a really bad state and she knew she was dying." Phoebe lifted her head to see the plains behind the wagons, memories flooding her thoughts. "She took my hand and told me to take good care of Grace. She said that Grace was so good and kind and that people might take advantage of her. She told me she was so proud of my strength and she knew I'd always keep my sister safe." Her voice caught as she remembered the moment in her mind.

"I promised my ma that I would always take care of her."

"Well, my dear girl, you have kept that promise. Some things are just out of your hands."

Still staring out beyond the wagons, Phoebe finally felt as though she had no more tears left to cry.

"When we were in St. Louis, after my pa died in the fire, our uncle took us in. I knew he was bad news but I didn't know what else to do. I knew we had to stay there until our brother got back but I'd taken a job and was saving money to get us out of there." She looked at the older woman who was still holding her arm around her shoulder.

"My uncle tried to hurt Grace in a way I would never have been able to forgive myself for. She shouldn't have had to deal with that fear. I should have got her away sooner." She dropped her eyes to the ground.

"Then, I agreed to drag her across the country to try getting her away safely and now she might not even make it."

Her voice choked on the last words and Susan pulled her close again.

"She's tougher than you give her credit for, Phoebe. I've watched that young slip of a girl work alongside you to care for the animals, making meals, and walking miles beside the wagon. And you've done everything and more than you needed to do for her and she knows it."

Standing up, Susan turned and dished up some bacon and biscuits sitting in the pan by the fire. "Now, you get eating so you can take care of your sister. I don't have any doubt that if anyone can beat an illness like this while out in the middle of nowhere, it's you two young ladies."

Just as Phoebe was about to eat, they heard a

commotion coming from the other side of the wagons.

"We have some ice! Colton knew there was a place around here that had underground stores of ice that were insulated and still frozen. Never seen the likes of it in my life! But he dug down and we found ice." James O'Hara was excited as he hopped off his horse with leather bags full of ice they'd found.

"Colton says to give this to Grace to help get her temperature down. We can also use it to make some nice cold drinks."

Colton had ridden up beside James, handing his bag down to the other man to take.

"How's she feeling today, Phoebe?" He held her gaze with concern in his eyes.

"She's the same. Still very hot but she did keep some water down early this morning."

Nodding, he rode his horse into the center of the wagons. The travelers all gathered around to see what the plan was going to be for the day. Some had already yoked their animals and packed up, ready to leave.

"We will be staying here another day. There are some ice stores just a ways from here and some of us will be going to get some more to bring back, if you'd like to come and replenish your water supplies. But keep your animals contained here so they don't get out too far. The ground just past here is not safe for animals to eat from or drink the water."

"We can't stay another day. We have to keep moving, and you know it, Colton."

Titus Cain walked up directly in front of Colton where he still sat on his horse.

"You're making a decision based on a sick girl who we all know likely isn't going to get better anyway. We need to keep moving and you're making a bad decision because of a woman."

Colton had hopped off his horse at the words Titus was saying, moving to stand directly in front of the other man.

"Are you questioning my authority, Titus?" He quietly spoke the words, leaving no doubt at the undercurrent of anger he was trying hard to control.

"I'm the one in charge on this wagon train. You all elected and hired me to get you safely to the Oregon Territory and that's what I intend to do, even though I would love nothing more than to leave you out here in the middle of these plains completely on your own."

Turning to face the others who were standing around, he continued. "Now, does anyone else have any concerns? We will stay here for the remainder of today, stock up on some water from the ice stores, and give the young woman who is fighting for her life in there the day to get better." He dared anyone else to argue.

Turning back to Titus, he spoke directly to him. "And you will back off. I will not have anyone questioning my decisions. We're still making good time and an extra day of rest won't hurt anyone. You are more than welcome to continue on by yourself."

Titus wasn't backing down.

"I might just do that." With that, he turned and stomped away. "I'm leaving. If anyone else would like to follow along with someone who doesn't let his feelings for a woman in a skirt get in the way, you're welcome to join me." He strode past where Phoebe was now standing beside Susan.

As he got next to her, he scowled. "Sorry about your sister but if you had any sense, you wouldn't let this outfit stop today because of you. There are already enough people questioning your reputation and now they'll be questioning Colton's authority as leader of this group."

Not sure what to say, Phoebe stood watching him storm away. She looked back and saw Colton still standing in the middle but the worst thing was, she could see a few of the others were already setting up to follow Titus.

CHAPTER 14

The relief from the setting sun was welcome to everyone. The day had been scorching, drying the ground almost instantly. Dust had started to settle all around them, sticking to the sweat that poured down their faces and bodies.

Grace was sleeping and had managed to keep water down since early this morning, so Phoebe was feeling much more optimistic. She was sure now it wasn't cholera.

The ice water had been a blessing and seemed to turn everything around. Laying the first chunk onto her hot forehead had brought such relief to her young face. Then, being able to drink the cool, fresh water seemed to be what made the difference.

In truth, everyone had been enjoying the freshness of the cold water after relying on warm, and not always clean, water for most of the journey.

Some of the families had mixed up some lemonade with a few lemons they had stashed in their supplies.

Those who had stayed enjoyed a day to rest and repair and had all pitched in together to help each other. It seemed that now there was no one around to argue and question every decision, the mood was much lighter.

Everyone had voiced concern for Grace and had taken the time to wish her well. Even Margaret and her mother Harriet had come over to see how she was feeling. Out of those who had stayed, it seemed they were thankful that perhaps if one of them were to become ill, Colton might make the same decision.

After Titus had left with a few others who'd decided to join him, Colton had come back and lifted Grace out of the wagon to put her in the shade underneath. Susan and Audrey had made a comfortable bed out of blankets for her to lie on and there was enough of a breeze to give her some relief.

Phoebe hadn't left her side throughout the day, pressing fresh ice water to her forehead and holding a cup to her lips as needed. The others had all taken turns helping with Grace, while the men in the outfit went with Colton to get as much ice as they could reasonably carry with them to refill their own water stores.

The air was turning crisp now with the sun gone and Phoebe could feel her stomach rumbling with hunger. Just as she was about to call out for Audrey who she could see over by the fire, she saw Colton walk up beside the wagon. He crouched down and peered under.

"How's she feeling now?" Phoebe felt so bad about the fact that people would be questioning his decisions because of her and her sister. But he'd never once made mention of it today.

She smiled down at her sister who was sleeping peacefully. "Her fever has broken and she hasn't brought up any water all day. I'm hopeful she has made it through the worst of it."

"I will put her back into the wagon now for the night. It's getting chilly out here and I think you could use a break to have something to eat."

Nodding her head, she let him pull on the blanket that Grace was laying on, then lift her into his arms. He stood and gently carried her sister to the back of the wagon and she noticed Grace open her eyes to smile at him.

"Thanks for letting me rest today, Mr. Wallace." Her voice was weak still but the color was starting to come back to her face.

Colton gave her the biggest smile Phoebe had ever seen. "I've told you to call me Colton. I'm not a mister." He bent his head closer to whisper. "And besides, I'd do anything for the prettiest girl out here on this trail."

Grace was beaming and Phoebe thought her heart would burst.

Audrey came over and put her hand on her shoulder. "I will go in and get her settled. You can take a break. I think the worst is over." Her friend smiled at Phoebe as she pushed her toward a crate by the fire.

Susan handed her a plate of food. "We'll be back on the trail by morning, so you get yourself filled up and then some sleep. We don't need you collapsing from exhaustion next."

"Thank you, Susan, and you too, James. You've both been so good to me and Grace ever since we started this journey." She meant every word. The older couple had taken them under their wing and always helped when needed.

Today, they'd both done what they could to help. She'd seen James help Colton with making some repairs on her wagon. She knew he'd gone back and helped get ice to fill up her own water stores.

Susan had never been too far away either.

"Sometimes, you've just got to learn to let yourself rely on others. Me and my James would do anything for you two girls." She handed Phoebe a cold glass of lemonade one of the other families had brought over. She stopped right in front of her, watching Phoebe's face as she continued. "Much like I believe Mr. Wallace would do."

Phoebe turned her head toward the wagon to make sure he hadn't heard and saw him jumping down from the back. He said something to Grace that she couldn't make out and she noticed the smile on his face as he spoke to her.

Turning, he raised an eyebrow as he noticed the two women staring at him. He slowly walked over to them by the fire.

"Did I miss something? Do I have horns growing out of my head?" Phoebe couldn't help noticing how tired he looked and she realized he'd faced a huge burden today, as well.

"No, Mr. Wallace, you don't have horns growing out of your head. But I'd imagine you are tired and hungry after the day you've had." Susan turned back to dish up some more food onto a plate. "I've seen how you haven't stopped today, fixing and fussing to make sure everyone is taken care of. So now you sit yourself down here beside Phoebe and the both of you get some food in your bellies."

Phoebe had to smile at the look on Colton's face. He, obviously, wasn't used to taking orders from anyone and he stood there not moving as though he wasn't quite sure what he was supposed to do.

He turned his eyes to Phoebe. She just shrugged

her shoulders as she popped a piece of biscuit into her mouth.

Colton sat down and took the plate from Susan's hands. Phoebe watched as he ate, realizing Susan was right. She hadn't seen Colton sit down once today while she'd been lying under the wagon with Grace.

He'd been busy working on repairs for her wagon, riding out to show the others where to find the ice, and had more than likely been spending his day trying to convince those who had stayed that he was still a leader they could trust.

As she watched him eating, she felt her cheeks heat as she remembered him holding her in his arms at the small makeshift grave on the trail. Quickly turning her eyes back down to her own plate before he caught her staring, she finished eating. Standing up, she went to where Susan was standing by the wagon, tidying up.

"Susan, you get yourself to bed. I will clean up. I need to stretch my legs a bit and would welcome having something to do for a while. Audrey is in with Grace, so I can finish up here. You've done more than anyone should have to do for us today, so please let me at least do this small bit for you." Smiling at the other woman, Phoebe took the cleaning cloth from Susan's hands.

The older woman reached out and hugged Phoebe. "I will see you in the morning. Give me a holler if you need anything through the night." She squeezed Phoebe's shoulders then turned and went to climb into the tent with her husband. Knowing they would be back on the trail early in the morning, James could already be heard snoring.

Suddenly feeling uncomfortable when she realized her and Colton were alone, she busied herself cleaning off her plate. She jumped when he walked up behind her and set his plate down on the step of the wagon.

He reached out and took her hand, turning her to face him. They stood looking at each other for what seemed like an eternity.

"Thank you for doing what you did today, Colton." She swallowed hard, unsure how to thank him enough for everything. "I know making the decision to stay an extra day cost you a great deal."

He shrugged. "We will have to get back on the trail in the morning. I wish we could give Grace another day to get better but we will make sure she is as comfortable as possible when we head out." He let go of her hand he was still holding and turned to sit back down on the crate.

"Men like Titus Cain are always trying to cause trouble. He wasn't happy about me being hired on to lead the wagons in the first place. He'd assumed he would be the one voted to be in charge." He leaned back and rested against the side of the wagon.

"Yes, but what if now the others start questioning you because of what he has said?" She went over and sat next to him. "I feel responsible. You've had to take care of us, something you had never agreed to in the first place. Because of us, now others are questioning your leadership."

He just sat staring at her with his arms behind his head, relaxing like he didn't have a care in the world. She wanted to kick his boots to see if he was even listening to what she was saying.

Finally, just as she was about to follow through on her thoughts, he smiled. "Phoebe, I'm a grown man. I can say yes or no without anyone making me do anything I don't want to do. The same goes for anyone else in this outfit. I make no secret that everyone is welcome to give their input about what we should do as a group. But the final decision goes to me. That's what I was hired to do. Most of the men here respect that and I respect them. Titus Cain was never one to offer any suggestions, only complaints."

He sat up, leaning his arms on his legs as he stretched out his back.

"Most of the people here know that, so anything he said today fell on deaf ears. The ones who chose to follow him will most likely be regretting that decision by now."

She wanted to tell him what Titus had said about others talking about her and questioning her reputation but she wasn't sure how to say it. Instead, she sat looking at her hands, trying to find the right words.

Colton reached out and took her hands in his. "Want to tell me what else is bothering you? You know your sister is likely out of the woods now. She will be all right."

She sat staring at his strong, worn hands holding hers. She knew her own hands were full of blisters and weren't the kind of delicate hands men liked to hold. But for some reason, she couldn't move them.

"I know. Thanks to you, Grace will likely have a chance to get better. I don't think she could have fought whatever was making her sick without having this day to rest."

"So, if you know she's getting better, what else is bothering you? I can tell something else is eating at you, Phoebe. And you normally don't have any trouble telling exactly what's on your mind." He tried to joke with her to get her to open up.

"It's just that I don't want you risking the others, or making decisions because of me."

She knew that didn't sound like what she wanted to say.

Colton let go of one of her hands and reached out to tilt her head up to look at him. His hand lingered, moving up to caress the skin by her jaw, then upward to gently touch her cheek. She could feel the calluses on his hands as they brushed her skin.

"Phoebe, I make decisions based on what is best for everyone. I knew we could afford the day to stop and rest." He was looking into her eyes so intently, she felt like she was frozen in place.

"I'm not the kind of man who will make someone suffer just to make good time. I would have done it for anyone." He was still touching her cheek and she was sure she could hear her heart beating.

She hated to break the moment but she had to tell him what Titus had said.

"Colton, I think you should know what some of the people are saying. They think you're making bad decisions because of me." She swallowed hard as he kept his eyes on hers. She felt like she couldn't speak above a whisper. "They are questioning my reputation."

He still hadn't moved, one hand holding hers and the other with his thumb gently making circles that left her skin tingling on her cheek. His blue eyes stared into hers. The only indication that he'd even heard her was the clenching she could see in his jaw below the stubble that covered it.

Before she had time to react, he was leaning toward her and she felt his lips on hers. His hand went back and pulled her head closer. She could feel his hand tangle in her hair, caressing the soft curls that fell down past her shoulders.

His lips gently moved on hers and she felt like the world around her was spinning. As soon as it had started, he sat back and let his hands fall. Standing up, he walked away before turning back to her.

She watched as he stood wrestling with what to say. He took his hat off and ran his hands through his thick black hair. "I'm sorry, Phoebe. I shouldn't have done that."

She still hadn't quite caught her breath, her chest still heaving with the emotions of what had just happened.

"I promise that your reputation will be completely safe with me. I will make sure the others don't ever see anything to question otherwise." He pushed his hat back on his head. "Now, you better get in and make sure Grace is sleeping. You need your rest so we can get on the trail early."

With that, he turned and walked away. She watched his retreating back until he was lost in the darkness of the night. Putting her fingers to her lips that were still tingling, she couldn't move.

She knew he'd promised to protect her reputation but after what just happened, she wasn't sure that's what she even wanted.

CHAPTER 15

"Pull the lines! Keep them tighter or you'll lose them!" Colton shouted to the men working to bring a few of the remaining livestock across the river. The animals were terrified, pulling against the ropes holding them and losing their footing as they fought the current.

Colton had been back and forth numerous times already today, helping to get the teams across, making sure everything was secure before starting the arduous crossing. He knew the Snake River could be difficult but at least this crossing wasn't as bad as it would've been if they tried crossing further up.

Here, they had to cross a stretch that had three small outcroppings in the water, getting them out of the water for a few moments before continuing for the next stretch. It had taken a full day to get half of the wagons across yesterday and today they were bringing the rest.

He'd explained to the men and women in the outfit that they could stay on the south side of the river and follow it along but the trail would be longer and harder on everyone.

The north side offered lush grass that would be welcome to the starving livestock, giving them a better chance of reaching the end of the trail. Since the water wasn't as high as it could be, they had the option to cross here, then cross back again further up the trail, giving everyone a better trail to follow.

He'd explained the dangers, holding his own misgivings and bad memories in check, while he let the others decide what they wanted to do.

Most of the others had immediately recognized the need to get across the river even if it was dangerous.

A few had been worried, feeling they would rather not take any chances. After taking a vote, they were given the option to continue along the south path and hopefully meet up at the other end to complete the journey with the rest of the group. But after what had happened the last time others had gone on ahead without the rest, none of them were willing to risk it.

After Titus had led the few other wagons away

when Grace was ill, they hadn't made it very far before some of the livestock had started to die. Not having taken Colton's warning to heed, they had allowed the livestock to eat the grass and drink water around the areas that were well known for killing animals.

Within a few days, they'd made the decision to wait for Colton and the others to catch up. The few men that had left with Titus had apologized profusely, vowing to follow the decisions he made from then on, without question.

Except for Titus. He'd been furious that the others had decided to go against him and wait for Colton. When the rest of the wagons had caught up to them, Titus hadn't spoken a word to anyone. He silently fumed to himself but Colton had no doubt he was still intent on making the trip difficult for everyone.

Looking to the wagons that were left to take across, he couldn't help but feel his eyes being drawn to the redhead walking around her wagon. Grace was sitting outside on the ground, leaning against the wheel. She was looking much better now but still struggled to walk very far.

It had been a few weeks now since she'd been sick and since the night outside the wagon with Phoebe, he'd gone out of his way to keep his distance. He knew the others were questioning what was happening with him and Phoebe, noticing how he always seemed to end up around their wagon for one reason or another.

He didn't want to cause any question about her reputation. If not for the fact that he had no intention of settling down, or staying in Oregon, he might be inclined to vie for her attention and see what could happen between them but he knew it wouldn't be fair to her.

He couldn't go home and he didn't think she would appreciate being dragged around the country with him for the rest of her life.

So, he knew he had to stay away for both of their sakes.

But it was hard. Colton noticed Titus was always hanging around her now that he wasn't nearby to keep an eye on her. He was sure Phoebe wouldn't be taken in by any of his false charm but he was still worried to see the other man paying attention to her.

He'd purposely made sure the other man's wagon was one of the first to cross yesterday, leaving him on the other side of the bank all night, while Phoebe was still back here.

Even though Colton had spent the evening listening to the incessant chatter of Margaret MacGregor and her mother who'd invited him for the evening meal, he'd kept his eye on the other wagon that held the woman he couldn't stop thinking about. He knew James and Susan would take care of them but he wanted to be nearby too, just in case.

"All right, boss! Just a few more wagons to get across. We'll be back on the trail by tomorrow morning!" Colton watched the back of the young man who was his top scout working with him. He had to smile at the exuberance he had for every task he did, even after weeks on the trail.

He kicked his heels into his own horse to catch up and get back across the water to the remaining wagons. He rode up to the three wagons he was taking across next, stopping by Phoebe's.

"Have you got all of your belongings secure? The water is shallow enough to pull the wagons across with the team hitched. I'll ride alongside on my horse. We will tie you together, three wagons across, with the O'Hara's and the MacGregors. Young Davis over there will take up the other side to keep the three teams corralled." He pointed to the young scout who was already helping the MacGregors get their belongings secured.

He hopped off his horse, not even glancing at Phoebe as he spoke. He didn't want to admit how scared he was to be taking her across.

Flashbacks to his father drowning in this exact spot had his stomach in knots and knowing he had to get Phoebe and Grace across scared him more than he wanted to admit.

"We will have a few other men on horseback

bringing up the flank, so if anything comes loose, or starts to float away, we can try to save as much as we can. The three of you will ride in the back of the wagon and stay put until I get you all across."

He wanted to make sure they were ready before he headed to the O'Hara's to let them know the plan. Realizing none of the ladies had said anything as he'd busied himself checking their team, he stopped and finally looked to Phoebe who was standing with a hand on her hip and one eyebrow raised as she glared at him.

"You don't bother coming around to speak to us for days, then think you can charge in here giving us orders?"

It was his turn to raise an eyebrow. Leaning against the wheel, he put his foot up on one of the spokes. "That's exactly what I think I can do. Do you have a better plan for getting yourself across the river?"

He noticed her hands shaking as she fumbled to tie up some of the canvas around the wagon bed.

"That's fine, Mr. Wallace. We will do whatever you say." Grace came over and placed her small hand on his arm. "Phoebe's just nervous, that's all." She smiled up at him.

"I've told you to stop calling me Mr. Wallace." He smiled back down at the girl.

She was going to break someone's heart some-day, he had no doubt about that. But right now, he had to deal with her older sister whose mood indicated she wasn't particularly happy with him at the moment.

He walked over to where Phoebe was pulling on the canvas, while the others turned to put the last few belongings into the wagon. Reaching out to help her, his hand brushed hers. He noticed her pull her hand away like he'd burned it.

"Listen, Phoebe. I'm sorry I haven't been around much. But you need to listen to me so I can get you safely across this river." He tugged the strap tight. "I don't want to lose anyone else to this water."

He quickly turned to throw a large crate into the back without giving her a chance to reply.

He helped Audrey climb into the back, then took Grace's hand to boost her up to take Audrey's hand. Once they were in, he turned to see where Phoebe had got off to. He was surprised to see her standing there beside him.

"I thought I was going to have to track you down to convince you to get in the back of this wagon." He offered her a smile. He knew she was likely just as confused as he was and it had probably stung to be ignored after sharing that kiss.

She just stood looking at him, making him uncomfortable.

"I know today is very difficult for you after what happened to your father at this crossing. So, I won't make it any harder for you." She lifted her chin, then reached her hand out so he could help her up. "But I'm not going to pretend to be happy you're here."

Ah, now that was his Phoebe. The one who could be sweet as pie then spitting fire all within one minute. He had to smile into the blue eyes staring back at him.

Helping her into the wagon, he went around and took the reins to start the team toward the bank. The O'Haras and MacGregors were following right behind. He could hear Margaret's high-pitched wailing at the thought of having to cross the river.

He hoped they would all get across without incident but he knew the river was unpredictable and, just because things had gone smooth yesterday and so far today, it didn't mean it was going to be like that now.

When they neared the bank, he got the three wagons to line up side by side. The men all worked together to secure the wagon beds tightly together. The O'Haras were in the middle, so they unhitched their team, leaving their wagon to go through using the strength of the other teams. Too many animals that close together would be dangerous in the water.

The sun beat down on the wagons sitting on the bank and a gentle breeze blew in the air. The wagons creaked as they waited their turn. The water flowing past sounded gently soothing to the people waiting to cross. They'd crossed many small rivers along the way without any problems.

But this river seemed different and it caused everyone to be a little more anxious. Colton checked everything over one more time before climbing onto his horse. He cringed to see one of the men who'd be flanking the wagons was Titus. He'd hoped some of the other men would come but he figured Titus had something to prove.

He moved to the back of the MacGregor wagon to ask if they were ready.

"Oh, Mr. Wallace. I'm so afraid." Margaret was sitting in a heap of fabric in the corner of the wagon. "And, I have so many priceless things that just can't be replaced. Promise me we won't lose anything!"

"Wish I could make that promise Margaret but you all know the risks involved with river crossings. This one is no different."

Harriet sat fanning herself, looking like she was going to burst. "Well, we need to get moving. The heat in this wagon is more than I can stand!"

Colton nodded his head then moved to the O'Hara wagon.

"We're all ready to go, Colton. Just give the word." Susan smiled out at him from her wagon. The woman was always smiling.

"You take good care of those girls in that wagon,

you hear me?" She pretended to scold him but he knew she genuinely was worried about the three ladies in the wagon beside her.

Nodding his head, he moved to Phoebe's wagon. Grace was huddled up beside Phoebe and Audrey was on the other side of her. Phoebe looked up at him with determined eyes.

"We know you'll get us safely across, Colton. We're ready."

He kicked his horse to take his position on the other side. Yelling out to the others, they all replied that they were ready. The wagons started to creak and groan as the animals moved toward the water. They were already starting to strain against the weight and when they stepped into the water, it was difficult to keep their footing.

Colton kept his eyes ahead, checking to the side as needed to make sure they were all still moving together. The first bit of the crossing went smooth, and they were soon finding themselves back in the water for the second stretch of river.

The animals were heaving and snorting, pulling hard against the current. The sound of the water hitting the sides of the wagons seemed to beat louder than he ever remembered. Finally, they were on the bank of the last outcropping. Just one more stretch of river to get through and these wagons would be safely across. He almost felt like he could breathe.

As the wagons made their way into the water, one of the lead oxen lost its footing, stumbling forward. Phoebe's wagon tilted dangerously as Colton watched helplessly. As though he was watching through a haze, he saw it right itself, at the same time he heard a large cracking sound.

The wagon had tilted too far back, hitting the side of the O'Hara's wagon, snapping one of the wheels with the force.

Unsure what damage had happened, he motioned for the rider behind him to move up and take his place in the line. He fell back as the others kept the wagons moving. Suddenly, he noticed James frantically yelling back as he stood on his bench at the front of the wagon.

Too late, Colton noticed Susan had tumbled from the back of the wagon. He hadn't heard her scream above the noise the wagons and oxen up front had been making. She was being dragged along with the current, desperately trying to keep her head above the water with her heavy skirts weighing her down.

As he leaped from his horse, he felt something hit his leg. Looking down, he was immobilized with fear as he saw Phoebe was in the water too, swimming and hollering to the other woman.

His heart sank in his chest, memories flooding back to the last time he was in this river. He dove in after her, reaching out to grab for her dress as she was swept away.

Feeling his grip miss the fabric, he watched in horror as Phoebe and Susan were both dragged and pulled further down the river.

CHAPTER 16

Her skirts were dragging her under, pulling her along with the swift current. Her hip banged into a rock, as she desperately fought to get her feet back under her. She hadn't even thought, jumping out of the wagon as soon as she'd seen Susan falling from the back of hers.

Now, she was regretting her decision. She should've let one of the men get Susan but her instincts had just taken over and fear of losing the woman who'd taken such good care of them on the trail, consumed her mind.

As hard as she tried, she couldn't get herself back upright, the current too strong as it drew her under, each time letting her up just long enough to catch a small breath. She knew she wouldn't have the strength to fight the water much longer.

She caught a glimpse of Colton's face as he raced

to catch up to her and she felt bad as she realized the guilt he would live with now. His eyes were full of fear and desperation. She could see his mouth moving as he called her name. Everything seemed to be moving slower than normal and his voice was barely reaching her ears.

Just when she thought maybe he'd be able to grab her arm the next time she came up for air, she felt her head strike against something under the water. Her last thought was of her sister and the promise she hadn't kept to her ma.

She could hear whispering around her but as hard as she tried, she couldn't open her eyes.

Someone was holding her hand and she felt a light kiss on the top of it. Wanting to see who was so worried, hoping to show them she was all right, she tried to talk. No words would come out and her eyelids felt like lead. No matter what she did, she couldn't tell them she was fine.

"Phoebe, I'm so sorry. I should have kept you with me. Why did you have to be so damn stupid? I would have got Susan. Why couldn't you have trusted me?" Colton's voice broke through her darkness, tearing at her heart as she heard the sadness in his words.

Trying to tell him it wasn't his fault, that she did

trust him, she desperately tried to open her eyes but the darkness overtook her again.

HER HEAD WAS THROBBING, sending jolts of pain with every beat of her heart. Afraid to open her eyes, knowing how much it was going to hurt, she decided to keep them closed. Opening her mouth to speak, hoping to ask for a drink, she startled herself at the weak moan that came out instead.

Instantly, she felt someone take her hand. Hoping it was Colton, she opened her eye a crack to peek out. Seeing her sister sitting beside her, eyes full of tears, helped her to get her eyes fully open.

Grace bent down, putting her small arms around her shoulders. "Phoebe, I was so scared you'd never wake up!" Her voice was coming out in broken sobs as the worry she had carried finally took over.

Not wanting to let on how much it hurt for Grace to be laying on her like she was, she gently put her arms around her sister's shoulders. "I'm fine, Grace. It would take more than a knock on the head to take me down."

Her sister leaned back and she noticed Audrey standing to the side. "What happened?" She couldn't remember anything since jumping in the river after Susan. "Oh no! Susan! Is she...?" She couldn't finish, fear of what she'd hear taking the words from her.

Audrey came over and patted her arm. "Susan's fine. The men were able to catch up with her further up the river. Titus actually saved her."

That surprised her. "Titus?"

Audrey smiled down at her. "After Colton grabbed you and dragged you out of the water, he was shouting orders at everyone. No one was going to argue with him at that point. The rest of the men managed to get the wagons across while some of the ones on shore raced along the bank. Titus rode his horse as far as he could, then jumped in and pulled Susan to safety."

"And Mr. Wallace carried you through the water, then brought you to the bank and sat holding you in his arms until we got here with the wagons." Grace finished the rest of the story, leaving no doubt by the sound of her voice that she believed Colton hung the stars in the sky.

Phoebe felt like her head was about to burst. Trying to sit up, she started feeling dizzy so had to lie back down. She could feel her face flush as the pain overtook her.

"Stay down, Phoebe. We aren't going anywhere, so just lie back and give yourself time to recover a bit." Audrey grabbed a cup with some water in it and helped bring it to her lips. The wetness instantly hit her dry throat, giving her much-needed relief. She let her eyes shut to block out the brightness of the sun beating down on her.

"Oh, Phoebe! My dear girl! What were you thinking?" Phoebe opened her eyes again when she heard Susan's voice. The older woman rushed over, kneeling down beside where Phoebe was laying on the ground. She wasn't even sure how but someone had laid out some blankets for her to lie on, keeping her off the dirt of the riverbank.

She gave the other woman a weak smile. "I wasn't thinking about anything, Susan. I saw you fall in and my instinct took over, telling me to get in and help you." She winced as the pain shot through her head. "I'll agree it might not have been the smartest decision I've made in my life."

"You're right about that, young lady. Oh, imagine my horror when I saw you jumping in behind me. Then, when they dragged me out of the river and I saw you laying here on this bank. I nearly collapsed from grief." She took a wet cloth Audrey handed her and patted it gently on Phoebe's forehead. "I could never have lived with myself if anything had happened to you."

Phoebe noticed tears in Susan's eyes. She reached her hand up and took the other woman's hand in hers, giving it a gentle squeeze.

"That's exactly the same thought I had when I saw you fall in the river, Susan. I only did what I had to do. I've already lost too many people I care about. I couldn't face losing you too." She could feel tears well up in her own eyes as she looked at the face that had become so dear to her over these weeks on the trail.

"Well then." Susan stood up and wiped her skirts. "There's a young man who's been beside himself with worry who has told us to let him know the minute you wake up." She turned, handing the cloth to Audrey.

Phoebe closed her eyes again, feeling the sun warm on her skin. The pain in her head was now just a dull throbbing, so she hoped she'd soon be able to get up. Her clothes were almost dry, so she wondered how long she'd lain here.

She heard footsteps and opened her eyes to see Colton standing gazing down at her. The worry on his face broke her heart.

He crouched down beside her, resting on one knee. "How are you feeling? Would it be too much for me to move you back into the shade of the other side of the wagon?"

She wouldn't admit it would most likely cause her some discomfort but she'd be grateful to be out of the sun, so she smiled at him and nodded. "I'm all right. I'd be happy moving into some shade, though." She went to sit up and cringed when the pain shot through again.

Colton reached out and put his arms beneath her shoulders and legs, gently lifting her from the ground. "Stop trying to do everything on your own and just let me help you for once."

"Audrey, Grace...grab the blankets and lay them on the other side of the wagon in the shade." He carried her carefully, as though she was breakable glass, and she had no choice but to reach her arms up around his neck. His face was so near hers, she could see the dimples in his cheek under the stubble.

Her hands touched the hair that hung below the back of his hat and as she found herself looking in his eyes, she remembered the fear she'd seen in them when she'd been in the water. She felt bad for the worry she had caused him.

"I'm sorry, Colton. I guess I made a bit of a mess of things today." She cringed as the pain shot through her head. She realized her whole body ached and the possibility of what could have happened today finally hit her. She'd risked so many lives today because of what she'd done, instead of just trusting that Colton or one of the others would be able to handle it.

She watched his jaw clench as he looked down at her. "Phoebe, I know you've been left to look after so much on your own but, sometimes, you have to just trust and let other people help. I would never have let Susan drown without trying to help her and neither would any of the other men riding in the water today." He swallowed hard.

"When I saw you getting dragged down that river, I've never felt fear like that in my life."

He kept gazing down at her and she could feel tears building in her eyes. She leaned her head into his chest so she didn't have to see the pain in his eyes, wrapping her fingers around the opening of his shirt.

By now, the girls had the blankets laid out nicely in a shady spot near the back of the wagon. Colton bent down and gently laid her back on the ground. As he took his hands out from under her, he reached up and pushed back a curl that had dropped into her eyes. She thought he wanted to say more but Grace came over and took a spot beside her on the ground.

Phoebe looked into his eyes and realized how much this man had come to mean to her. He'd been there to help whenever she needed it and even when she didn't think she did.

He stood up, turning to Audrey and Susan. "I'll be back in a while to check on her. Just keep her comfortable and let me know if you need anything." With that, he walked away behind the wagon.

Audrey watched him walk away, then came over to her. "Well, if I didn't know better, I would say that man is hopelessly in love with you." Her grin covered her face as she turned to work on putting food together for the evening meal.

Was Audrey right? And, how did she feel about

Colton? She closed her eyes remembering the feeling of being in his arms, the look in his eyes as he'd carried her here. She remembered their kiss. As she did, her heart did a double beat.

She *did* love him. The thought scared her because she didn't know what to do now that she'd finally admitted it to herself. The man she had come to know still seemed to hold himself back from her and she couldn't understand why.

If he did love her, why didn't he tell her?

CHAPTER 17

Colton reached down, dipping his hat in the cool water streaming past. He took one hand and cupped it to bring it up and wash the dust from his face. He was crouched down at the edge of the bank, trying to get his emotions back under control after the events of the day.

Watching Phoebe struggling in the water had torn him apart. When he'd finally grabbed her hand, after she'd struck the large rock under the water, he felt like the world had stopped. Looking at her face, eyes closed and no longer aware of anything around her, he'd thought he was too late.

When he got to the bank with her in his arms, he hadn't noticed anything else going on around him. He'd sat there holding her in his arms, wiping the hair from her eyes while the rest of the men got the wagons across. He'd glanced up once to see

Titus carrying Susan in. The woman was still conscious and was screaming for Phoebe.

He'd sat holding Phoebe's hand, whispering to her, begging her to wake up. He knew the others had seen him but he didn't care. When they brought her wagon up, the women had busied themselves getting blankets on the ground for her. Realizing they could look after her, he had reluctantly laid her down and let them take over.

He still had to help bring the last few wagons across and now everyone was spooked from what had happened. The rest of the afternoon had been tiring, worrying about getting everyone safely across, while his mind kept going to the woman lying on the ground beside her wagon.

"How's she doing?" Colton jumped at the sound of the voice beside him. He turned his head to see Titus leaning down cooling himself with the fresh water too.

"She took a hard knock to the head on that rock but she's awake now and, other than a bit of a headache, I think she'll be all right."

"Good to hear." Titus kept his eyes staring back across the river.

Colton struggled to find the words to continue. "Thanks for your help today. Not just with rescuing Susan, but the help getting the wagons across." He looked out across the river too. "Couldn't have done it without you."

The other man shrugged. "Just doing what anyone would have done."

As they sat there in silence, listening to the sounds of wagons creaking, animals moving around, and people talking, a rider on a horse appeared just on the other side of the bank.

"Who's that? We didn't leave anyone over there, did we?" Titus put his hand up to shield his eyes to see if he could recognize him.

Colton did the same but the figure was still too far away to see who it was. They stood to watch as the man started crossing.

By the time he was halfway across, Colton knew exactly who the rider was. And he wasn't going to be happy to see the state his sister was in.

"So, do you want to tell me exactly what is going on with you and my sister?" Luke Hamilton had ridden in like a tornado earlier. He'd spent the first hour growling at him for letting his sister get hurt, then finally accepting that she was going to be all right and maybe it wasn't entirely Colton's fault.

Grace had been stuck to his side since he arrived, so happy to finally have her older brother around again.

Now, the two men were sitting around the fire,

everyone else having long ago gone to their beds for the early start in the morning.

Colton kept his eyes on the fire, unwilling to give anything away by looking at his friend. "What makes you think anything is going on?"

Luke laughed. "Seriously? It's as obvious as the eyes on your head. Sorry to say my friend, you can't be saved." His grin covered his whole face as Colton glared at him.

He stared at his friend with a scowl, making sure he knew exactly what he thought about the topic of their conversation.

He decided it was best to change the subject. "How did things go in St. Louis?"

Luke stared at him with the smile still reaching across his face, obviously aware of Colton's refusal to discuss Phoebe any more. Finally, he shrugged and looked back toward the fire.

"Not as well as I'd hoped but at least my sisters are away from that man. I have no doubt he had something to do with my father's death but there's no way to prove it." He lifted his head to look at Colton. "Did Phoebe ever mention what happened?"

"She hasn't really told me much." Colton realized she hadn't ever confided to him what all had happened to force them on this trek across the country.

He watched as Luke tightened his fists, trying to

control the anger that was obviously brewing as he thought about it.

"That lecherous swine had bad intentions toward Grace and let's just say that if not for Phoebe and her ability to handle a gun, he may have got away with it." Luke hissed the words out between clenched teeth.

"And, this was after he tried to marry Phoebe off to one of his disgusting excuses for a friend, for a small fee." Luke stopped to smile. "Of course, that man wanted nothing to do with her after she gave him a taste of her feistier side. But that just made our uncle even angrier and more difficult for them to live with."

Luke looked down at his hands gripped together hanging over his knees. "They should never have been left on their own. I should've been there for them when our parents died."

Colton knew the guilt the other man carried. "We all have our demons and the guilt we have to bear. Sometimes though, we have to realize we did the best we could and not everything is our fault."

Luke lifted his head and raised an eyebrow as he glanced at Colton. "Kind of like carrying the guilt of a father's death that couldn't have been helped? The kind of guilt that keeps you away from a family who loves you?"

"It's more than that and you know it Luke." Colton wasn't in any mood to discuss his own issues.

"Oh right...the fight with your brother over a woman. You'd seriously throw away a relationship with your brother over a girl you never really loved anyway? Because I think we both know you only ever had any interest in her because you knew it made your brother angry."

Colton glared at Luke. The other man put his hands up in surrender. "Hey, I know, none of my business. Like you said...we all have our own demons we carry with us. I just thought, by now, you'd have realized how important family is. I'd give anything to go back and have another chance to make things right with my pa. But I won't get that chance. And, if you aren't careful, you'll miss your chance to make things right with your brother."

Luke stood up and patted him on the back. "Well, I've had a long day in the saddle and from what I hear, you run a tight operation and will be leaving before sunup."

Colton sat watching the other man walk away. Why did Luke always have to make so much sense? He just wasn't sure if he was ready to let go of the years of guilt and anger he'd been holding on to.

Pushing his hand through his hair in frustration, he got up and went to his bedroll. He knew he wasn't going to get much sleep, worry about Phoebe still eating at his thoughts. And now, thanks to Luke, he had even more thoughts to keep him awake long into the night.

CHAPTER 18

Her head wasn't aching as bad today as previous days, so Phoebe hoped she'd be back to normal soon. There was still a nice big lump where her head had made contact with the rock but the bluish bruise was starting to fade.

They'd stopped at Fort Boise yesterday and spent the day getting stocked up for the final leg of the journey. Tomorrow, Colton had told them, they'd reach the point where they would have to cross back over the Snake River. His eyes had found hers as he'd shared the news with the others.

Nerves were on edge and tempers were being fueled by the intense heat of the day and the weariness of the travelers. The worry of crossing the river played on everyone's minds, even with Colton's assurances that for this crossing, the Indians in the area would be there to help them. She wasn't sure if that helped ease everyone's worries or made them worse. Even though they'd made the journey without incident, there was always talk about the possibility of attacks by Indians. However, from what Phoebe had witnessed from the few they had met along the way, they had nothing to worry about.

"We've decided to have a bit of a party tonight, Phoebe, to celebrate you feeling better and to try and ease some of the tension that is building about this next river crossing." Susan bustled over to where Phoebe was hanging the pot over the fire to make coffee.

They'd managed to get a few potatoes at the Fort, and some other rations of meat and vegetables, and everyone was excited for a delicious stew after weeks of bacon and biscuits. Audrey was already cutting up some of the vegetables, while Grace shook out some of their clothes at the back of the wagon.

"That sounds wonderful, Susan." She smiled at the other woman who was obviously excited over the thought of having a party. Over the weeks on the trail, now and then, they would just get together to spend the evening celebrating the fact that they'd made it this far. The entire group that had set off from Independence all those weeks ago had become like a family.

Well, most of the families had. The MacGregors still kept pretty much to themselves, except to insist on having Colton for meals as often as they could. Margaret was still complaining non-stop about the heat, the dust, the walking...everything she hated about this trip.

"I'm going to make some dessert with some strawberries I picked up at the Fort!" Susan was so excited, it made Phoebe smile. The woman just loved to visit and be around other people. Phoebe worried about what would happen at the end of the trail in Oregon Territory. Now that her brother was here, it hadn't been discussed what they'd do when they got there.

She truly hoped he didn't plan on turning around and taking them back to St. Louis in the spring. Not only did she dread the thought of spending more weeks on this trail, she had a niggling thought that she'd miss Colton. Not that she would admit that to her brother though.

Since the day she'd been saved from the river, Colton had stayed close but she wondered if that was because of her or if it was just because Luke was back around. She knew they had a strong friendship and it would make sense he'd be happy to spend time with her brother.

She'd caught him watching her many times but they never had a chance to be alone, so she still wasn't sure what his feelings were. The more she had time to think, she'd realized she was definitely in love with him. It scared her to finally admit it, especially since she didn't know what the future would hold.

"Are you going to leave anything left on that potato to go in the pot?" She jumped as the voice belonging to the man she was thinking about spoke right behind her.

She looked down at the sliver of the potato she held in her hands. While she'd been lost in her thoughts, she'd peeled it back to the size of a bean.

She turned and saw Colton leaning against the wagon bed. He smiled at her and she thought she would drop the knife she was holding in her hand. How did he manage to have this kind of effect on her?

"How have you been feeling?" He pushed himself away from the wagon and came over to her. Reaching up, he brushed her hair back to show the bruised lump on her forehead. He examined it intently, and as she watched, she noticed his jaw clench.

"Still looks pretty bruised but I think it's getting better. I don't have the headache as much anymore." She felt every inch of her body tingle as he stood this close to her.

His hand dropped to her shoulder, then slid down her arm. "I'm glad." He smiled at her as his hand finally stopped on hers.

"I have something I wanted to give you. It might even cover what's left of the bruise." He looked at her nervously, then reached into his vest and pulled something out that was wrapped in tissue.

She looked at it, then up to his face. "What is it, Colton?"

He smiled. "You'd find that out if you opened it." He placed the package in her hands.

She ripped the paper off, seeing the most beautiful fabric folded inside. She yanked it out, realizing it was a bonnet in the deepest green color she'd ever seen. The fabric was soft and as she held it, her fingers rubbed it lovingly.

Her eyes lifted to his. She wanted to ask him why he would buy her something so beautiful but her voice was choked. He just lifted his shoulders and smiled. "You traded your good bonnet for a necklace for your sister. I know it was likely your best one, so I wanted to get you a new one. I saw this one at the Fort and thought it would look nice on you."

She had to put her eyes back down so he wouldn't see the tears.

"Am I interrupting anything?" Luke's cheerful voice broke through the spell Phoebe was under. She lifted her head and had to smile at the look of frustration on Colton's face at the sound of her brother walking up behind them.

"Not at all, Luke. As usual, you have perfect timing." Colton turned and scowled at Luke. "Just checking to see how your sister is feeling."

"Oh, right! A good wagon train boss needs to check on all of his charges." He gave them an exaggerated wink.

Colton turned to face her. "I'll see you later at the party." Then, he walked past her brother without another word.

"Luke, why do you always seem to know how to annoy everyone? I thought it was just me who was lucky enough to deal with you but I see you have that effect on everyone." She smiled as she scolded her brother.

He just shrugged. "Sorry, Phoebe. Colton's my friend but until he proves to me that he has honorable intentions, and figures out exactly what he wants in his life, I won't be letting him anywhere near my sister." He popped a raw carrot into his mouth.

"I kind of thought the two of you would hit it off, that's part of the reason I wanted you disguised in the first place. I foolishly hoped it would keep his interest elsewhere. Colton isn't ready to settle down and as much as I'd do anything for him, I won't let him hurt my sister."

Phoebe shook her head at her brother. Ever since they were little kids, he'd been overprotective of her.

"I would have thought you'd have figured out by now that I'm a grown woman who can take care of myself." She set the bonnet down on the ledge of the wagon, then went back to cutting the vegetables.

Thankfully, Grace ran over and Luke grabbed her in a big bear hug. "What have you been up to, Peanut?" Phoebe smiled at the expression Luke had used, not likely even realizing it was the same endearment her father had used for Grace.

Grace was finally completely recovered and since there was so much help between Audrey, Susan, and now Luke, Grace was finally able to let go of some of the responsibilities she'd been faced with for most of the journey.

"Just helping to set out some things for the party. Everyone is so excited! We can dance Luke!" She worshipped her brother and the thought of spending the evening dancing with him had put a smile on her face.

Phoebe had a smile on her face too. She'd decided she was a big girl, no matter what her brother thought, and she planned to let Colton know how she felt. She glanced over at the gift he'd given her and she smiled to herself. She didn't know what would happen when they got to the end of the trail but she had to take a chance.

She'd lost too many people in her life. This journey had taken people from them and almost took her sister too. Falling in the river and almost losing her life had made her realize she shouldn't wait to tell people how she felt.

And now that she finally knew how she felt, she had to tell him. She just hoped he felt the same.

❦

THE SOUND of the fiddle carried through the darkness of the night, along with the laughter and clapping of the people gathered between the wagons. They knew they still had a ways to go but, in their minds, they'd made it through so much already that they deserved a celebration.

Phoebe sat watching Audrey being swept around by one of the young scouts in the clearing they'd designated for dancing. Her friend smiled and was having fun but Phoebe could see the sadness in her eyes. Her mind went back to that night so many weeks ago when Audrey had been dancing with her husband, Pete. The next day, he had become sick and was gone before nightfall.

Her eyes found Grace and Luke dancing too. Her sister was beaming, having the time of her life. She tried not to notice Colton dancing with Margaret.

"How come you aren't up dancing with the others, dear?" Susan sat beside her, patting her hand as she sat down.

"I'm just going to take it easy tonight, Susan. My head is aching a bit, so I just want to be careful."

Her eyes found Colton once more, and she

could feel Susan squeeze her hand. "I'm sure he'd far rather be dancing with you." The older woman leaned in as she whispered to Phoebe.

She offered the other woman a smile as James joined them. She watched how he leaned down to kiss his wife like she was still a new bride. She could only hope to have a love like that someday.

Luke and Grace came over, talking and laughing. Luke tried to get Phoebe up for a dance but settled for Susan when she declined. She was waiting for a chance to talk to Colton alone and she'd noticed him walking to the other side of the wagons.

Excusing herself from James and Grace, she smiled as she saw the older man lead her sister out for a dance.

She made her way around the wagons, using the light from the fire and the full moon that hung in the sky. The stars seemed to go on forever when she looked up, feeling the coolness of the night breeze touch her face now that she was away from the warmth of the fire.

Hearing a sound just behind the MacGregor wagon, she headed that direction to find Colton. As she came around the corner, the light from a lantern illuminated the couple standing in an embrace.

Margaret was on her toes, kissing Colton, her hands around his shoulders with his hands on her waist. Phoebe's hand flew to her mouth, stifling the sob that threatened to escape.

Turning to run, she bumped into Titus who'd walked up behind her. "What are you doing back here by yourself, Phoebe?" His voice carried to the others and she heard Colton's steps as he came around the wagon.

"What the hell are you doing back here with him, Phoebe?" Colton was angry when he saw them standing there. All she could do was turn and look at him incredulously. As if he had any right to be accusing her of anything!

"What I do is none of your concern." With that, she turned to walk to her wagon where she could be alone. She felt Colton grab her arm. Pulling it away from him, she kept walking.

She could hear Titus telling him to let her go. They started arguing but, by then, she was too far away to hear. She crawled into her wagon, curled up in a ball with the blankets, and cried herself to sleep.

CHAPTER 19

Colton scanned the faces milling around the wagons for a sign of the one framed by the fiery red hair. He knew Phoebe was mad and he had a sinking suspicion he knew why.

After she'd stormed off, he'd blasted Titus for taking advantage of her. The other man had assured him nothing had happened and that he'd come across her as she was already running back to her wagon.

Titus had pointed out that he'd like nothing more than to have Phoebe alone in the dark but that she'd made it clear where her interests lay and they weren't with him.

Realizing the man would have rather enjoyed leaving him to think something had happened between him and Phoebe but had chosen to take the higher road, Colton was forced to believe him.

That meant she'd seen Margaret kissing him. He cringed inwardly as he recalled what had happened last night.

Margaret had asked him to help her open a chest she had, which kept a shawl she needed. The night had gotten cooler, so Colton had obliged. When they got to the back of the wagon, she'd turned on him before he knew what was happening, throwing herself into his arms.

In shock, he'd held her from falling as she reached up and started to kiss him. He assumed, from Phoebe's reaction, she had witnessed what happened. He felt terrible but if she wasn't so head-strong and had given him a chance to explain, he could have sorted it all out.

In fairness, he guessed he shouldn't have accused her of being with Titus. But seeing her out there alone with him had angered him, causing him to lash out without thinking.

Phoebe was making him crazy. If he was smart, he'd just let her go on thinking something had happened and get on with his life. Was he really ready to settle down, anyway?

Just last night, before everything happened, he'd decided he would go home and face his family. He'd face his brother and try to make things right. And, he'd decided he would take Phoebe with him.

Talking with Luke had made him realize what

was important and he'd witnessed so much of it during these past few weeks.

He couldn't imagine his life now at the end of this trail without Phoebe around. But now, he had to figure out how to make her see things his way. And, knowing her the way he did, he knew she wasn't going to make any of it easy for him.

They were crossing the river today, having arrived here early enough to get across before night-fall. With the help of the Indians who'd set up pulley systems to help them across, he knew it would be much quicker this time around.

"Not sure what you managed to do to rile my sister up but I reckon you better keep your distance from her if you know what's good for you." Luke swatted Colton on the back as he gave him a smug smile. He knew Luke wasn't particularly happy about what was happening between him and Phoebe, believing he wouldn't settle down and take care of his sister like she deserved.

"Don't worry about me, I can handle your sister." He glared at Luke, not in the mood for his comments.

Luke shrugged. "Suit yourself, but I warned you. She's angrier than a horse with a bee under the saddle." He turned and walked back toward the wagon. At least with Luke here, he could take control of Phoebe's wagon and get it across, leaving Colton with one less worry.

The wagons were lining up and some of the men had already formed groups to start taking the livestock across. He went to help, glad for something else to focus his thoughts on.

After they'd got them safely across, he turned and saw that the first few wagons were in the water, being guided easily by the pulleys. He noticed Phoebe's wagon sitting on the bank ready to be hooked up next. Luke was walking around, tightening ropes and straps and, as he watched, he noticed Phoebe standing, about to get in the back of the wagon.

She held her hands in front of her, and her head was high, but he could tell she was nervous.

Something inside him stirred, pushing him to get there and check everything for himself. Closing the distance, she noticed him coming and turned her head away. Seeing her do that, he knew what he had to do.

He smiled to himself because he also knew she wasn't going to like it.

PHOEBE TRIED to settle her nerves but the lack of sleep last night, along with the stress of standing about to cross the same river that had almost killed her, was making her a little on edge.

She'd seen Colton heading toward the bank of

the river and had turned her head so she wouldn't have to face him. She wasn't in the mood to be pleasant in front of the others.

"All right, sis. Let's get you up in the wagon." Luke's voice startled her. "Grace and Audrey are loaded up and I'll ride on the front seat so will be right here if anything goes wrong." She smiled at him, knowing that he understood her fears.

Before she had a chance to respond, she heard the splashing of hooves breaking through the edge of the water. "That's okay, Luke. I'm taking her across with me."

She whipped her head around and, without even waiting to see if she would agree, he'd reached down and was lifting her up onto the saddle in front of him.

"Colton! Put me down this instant! What are you doing?" She was furious, and if not for her fear of falling from the hold he had on her, she'd have hit him square on the jaw. "Luke, make him put me down!" She looked to her brother for help.

He was standing with one leg about to climb onto the wagon. "Sorry, Phoebe. Looks like Colton has things under control." She swore when she met up with him on the other side of the river, her brother was going to learn the extent of her vocabulary.

She glanced past him and noticed no one was stepping up to help her. Even Titus stood watching with a grin on his face at the scene Colton was causing.

He turned the horse around to start going back down the bank. "You're going to have to hold on Phoebe or you might find yourself back in the water." He smirked down at her, knowing she had no choice but to hold on to him.

Putting her hands around his neck, she resisted the urge to strangle him. She would wait until he got her safely across before giving in to that desire.

As they got into the deepest part of the river, she could feel the water pulling at her skirt that hung down below Colton's legs. Trying not to panic, she let Colton pull her tighter.

"I'm not going to let anything to happen to you, Phoebe. You have to trust me." His chest rumbled beneath her cheek as he spoke. His arms held her firmly in front of him.

His horse missed a step, stumbling forward. She let out a small cry, sure they were going to fall in again. He lowered his head as he righted the horse in the water. "I've got you, Phoebe. And I'm not letting go."

Finally, they made it to the other bank and she could pull her head out of his chest and look around. She saw her wagon coming across with Luke on the seat. She tried not to make eye contact with anyone else, embarrassment over having to be brought across on Colton's horse leaving her cheeks burning.

"You can let me down now." She tried to sit herself up, not meeting his eyes. She knew she'd let down her guard when they were in the water, allowing him to hold her close, but now that they were across, she wasn't prepared to stay sitting on his lap on top of his horse with all eyes on them.

"I could." He kept the horse moving past the few wagons that had already been brought over.

"Well, let me down then!" She pushed against his chest, trying to get him to stop.

"Phoebe. Just sit still. It's time you and I had a talk." With that, he kicked his heels into his horse and took off past some bushes on the other side of the camp.

"Colton! What will people think?" She looked back to where the people were setting up the camp on this side of the river where they would stay tonight.

"I'm sure most of them will be thinking it's about time I sorted things out with you. And, the rest of them, I don't care what they think."

"But you're the leader of this wagon train. You need to be there to get the wagons over and to take charge. Besides, I have nothing to say to you that we couldn't have said back at the camp."

She could feel his arms pull her closer as he leaned his head down. "Maybe what you had to say could be said back there but I promise you what I have to say, and what I have to do, is better left between us." He lifted his head back up as he stopped his horse by an opening with a small creek coming off the river. "Besides, I already talked with Titus. He is taking care of the wagons while I take care of you."

Phoebe didn't even know what to say. Her heart was pounding and she was sure if he set her down, she wouldn't be able to stand on her own. What was he planning to do?

CHAPTER 20

He put his hands on her waist, gently lowering her to the ground. "Well, that was much nicer than the manhandling I received getting dragged up onto your horse!" She busied herself brushing the dust off her skirts while Colton brought his leg over the saddle and dismounted.

She watched him nervously as turned to face her.

"I know what you think you saw last night, Phoebe." He walked over to her. "But if you'd stayed around and let me explain, you would have realized it wasn't what you thought."

"Why would I have stayed around when you seemed determined to accuse me of being there with Titus? Or did you forget that part?" She was trembling as the emotion of seeing Colton kissing Margaret came back to her mind.

He pulled his hat off his head, hitting it against his thigh as he looked down sheepishly. He brought his other hand up to rub his jaw. "I'll admit I may have reacted badly when I saw you there with Titus..."

"Reacted badly? Colton, you'd already made up your mind that I'd been on some secret tryst with Titus." He raised his eyebrow as he leveled his gaze on her.

"Much like you did with me and Margaret."

"No, not at all like that. I saw you kissing her. There's a big difference." She turned away from him and brought her hands up to hug her stomach. "Anyway, Colton, it doesn't matter. It's not like you and I have something going. What you do with other women is of no concern to me." She lifted her chin to look out at the river in the distance.

Colton walked up right behind her, placing his hands on her shoulders. "Phoebe. I wasn't kissing Margaret. She was kissing me. *That's a big difference*." He tugged on her shoulders to turn her back around.

Tears had formed in her eyes and she struggled to get her hands up to wipe them before he saw. "Phoebe, you're the only one I want to be kissing." With that, he brought his head down and covered her lips with his. His thumb caressed her cheek as he moved his lips gently on hers.

Lifting his head back, he kept his thumb

rubbing her cheek. "But I haven't been fair to you. All this time, I couldn't keep myself away but wasn't sure what I could ever offer you. And, I knew I had to protect your reputation among the others, so I tried my best to stay away." He leaned his forehead on hers. "But I couldn't do it. I can't stay away from you." He sounded pained as he said the last words.

"Your brother trusted me to take care of you and I had to do what I could to protect you. I never meant for this to happen." He lifted his head, peering down into her eyes. She forgot how to breathe as she saw the emotion in his blue eyes staring down at her.

"Never meant for what to happen, Colton?" She wasn't sure what he was saying.

He gave her a weak smile. "For me to fall in love with you." He waited, not moving as she registered what he'd said. She stood staring back at him, unable to speak.

A tear escaped from her eye and she watched as he bent down and kissed it from her cheek. His eyes were only inches away from hers and she could feel his breath on her mouth where he only lifted back far enough to see her face.

"I want to stay in Oregon, make things right with my family, and I want you to stay with me." His eyes hadn't left hers.

"Colton...I...I...I don't know what to say." She

could hear the beating of her heart in her head and everything around her was starting to spin.

He smiled down at her, again. "I find it hard to believe you would ever be at a loss for words." He brought both of her hands up between them. "I've put my heart out there, Phoebe, and I mean every word. So, all I need now is to hear what you have to say." She could see worry in his eyes that she might not feel the same way.

"Colton, you've helped me through so many trying times on this journey. You've always been there when I needed you and sometimes when I didn't want you to be." She offered him a smile that showed she knew how stubborn she could be at times.

"Last night, when I came to find you and saw you kissing Margaret, my heart felt like it had broken into a thousand pieces." She swallowed as she tried to find the words to continue. She reached one hand up to gently rub the stubble around his cheek, feeling the smile as it grew on his face.

"I'd been coming to tell you I loved you." She watched as his eyes darkened, then closed as he heard the words she'd spoken. He groaned then brought his lips back to hers, kissing her with an urgency she had never felt before.

When he lifted his head, he brought his hand up to brush her hair back. Before he could say anything more, a voice interrupted.

"Is everything all right here, Phoebe?" Her brother's voice brought a smile to her lips. Colton put his head back down on her forehead as he sighed.

"Luke, you really know how to ruin a moment." Colton groaned out as he lifted his head, smiling down at Phoebe.

"Well, I let you race off with her over your lap. I thought the least I should do is make sure she didn't need me to rescue her from you." Phoebe turned to see her brother sitting on his horse, grinning down at the two of them.

Turning back to Colton, she smiled. "No, Luke, I don't need rescuing. I'm exactly where I want to be."

Chuckling to himself, Luke turned his horse around and rode away.

Phoebe let Colton take her in his arms again. As he brought his head back down to hers, he whispered, "And I'm never letting you go."

She smiled, knowing that's all she'd ever wanted.

EPILOGUE

The sun sat high in the sky and a gentle breeze blew in from the north. The air was cool now with the approaching winter, blowing the hair from her face.

They brought their horses up to a stop at the end of the lane leading to the house set back in the trees. Phoebe glanced toward Colton, seeing the tension in his jaw as he looked at his mother's home. She understood his worry about coming home after being gone for so long as much as she understood the guilt and anger that had taken him away in the first place.

She reached over and squeezed his hand. "Are you ready?" He peered down at their hands and smiled.

He raised his eyes to hers. "I'm ready. Are you

sure you want to come with me? You could have stayed in town with the others."

A few of the families had chosen to stay in Oregon City for the winter, waiting until the spring to settle their claims. But some had followed Colton and Phoebe to the small settlement near where his family lived. Bethany was still growing but it was located in a perfect location between another settlement called Skinner's Mudhole and New Albany in the Willamette Valley.

They clicked their heels to get the horses moving toward the house. Phoebe had decided to ride Luke's horse, instead of dragging the wagon all the way out here. And she'd declined the offer of a side-saddle in town.

As they neared the house, a small woman with light brown hair and hints of grey walked out, shielding her eyes from the glare of the sun. Phoebe heard her cry out when she recognized the figure on the horse beside her. She smiled as Colton raced the rest of the distance, jumped down and swept his mother into his arms.

He spun her around and as Phoebe pulled up, she could hear the older woman sobbing. "Colton! I feared we'd never see you again!" Phoebe sat back, letting them have their reunion.

The woman was holding Colton's face in her hands, covering it with kisses as she cried.

"Ma! I'm fine." Colton laughed as he held his

mother back from him. Finally, the woman spotted Phoebe sitting on the horse. "I have someone I'd like you to meet."

He came over and reached up to lift Phoebe down. He put his arm around her shoulders, leading her to where his mother stood. "Ma, this is Phoebe. We're getting married." Phoebe had to laugh at the shocked expression on the other woman's face as he blurted the news out.

"Phoebe, this is my ma, Anna Wallace."

His mother reached out, pulling Phoebe in for a hug. "Well, I can't imagine what lies he would have told you to convince you to marry him but I'm awful glad to meet you!"

Phoebe liked her immediately. She could see Colton tense as his gaze moved toward the house. His mother noticed too, turning and smiling. "Colton, your brother is here visiting. I know he'll be glad to see you." A man that resembled Colton had walked out and was standing on the porch.

But before he could speak, a woman pushed past him and ran out the door. "Colton!" Phoebe felt her body tense as the other woman threw herself into his arms. He was laughing, lifting her off the ground and spinning her around. Phoebe assumed this was the woman the brothers had fought over, causing Colton to leave.

Her face must have given her away because

Colton dragged the other girl over, who was still clinging to him like her life depended on it.

"Phoebe. This is Ella. My twin sister." Phoebe found herself letting the air out of her lungs she hadn't even realized she was holding. His twin sister!

She smiled at the woman who'd finally let go of Colton long enough to notice her.

"Thank you for dragging this sorry excuse for a brother home. You have no idea how much I've missed him, even if he does annoy me." The woman Phoebe was looking at was beautiful and she could see how much she'd missed her brother. She could understand.

She smiled, offering her hand. "Oh, I think I have a pretty good idea what it's like to miss a brother, even if he drives you crazy."

By now, the man on the porch had made his way over. "Colton."

Colton turned and faced him. "Reid." Everyone else just stood waiting for them to say something else. In the silence, more voices came from the house. As Phoebe stood watching, two more figures ran from the house, one holding a small child. When they got to where the crowd had gathered, the boy handed the baby to Reid.

They gathered around Colton, slapping him on the back and laughing with him. Phoebe assumed these were the other brothers, Logan and Connor, who he'd told her about.

When it was all over, Colton turned back to Reid. He reached out and gave his finger to the baby to grab hold of. He smiled down at the child, then looked up at Reid with a question in his eyes.

"This is my daughter, Sophia." Reid smiled down at his little girl lovingly. Colton laughed as she pulled his finger into her mouth.

Colton brought Phoebe over beside him. "Reid, this is Phoebe. The woman who stole my heart and has convinced me it's time to settle down." Phoebe gave him a glance that indicated she didn't approve of him making her sound like she was tying him down.

But she figured since he was likely trying to make sure his brother understood there were no hard feelings over the woman they'd fought about all those years ago, she would let him get away with it this time.

Reid looked at her intently and she realized the bright blue eyes must be a thing in this family. He watched her for a while, then nodded as he put his hand out to her.

"All right! Phoebe, you must come in and sit down. I want you to tell me everything!" Colton's mom started herding the group toward the house, taking the baby from Reid's arms. Ella put her arm through Phoebe's, leading her up the steps.

Reid and Colton stayed back and Phoebe realized the others had known they needed some time alone. She smiled to see the love a family like this would have for each other. She hoped Colton and Reid could work everything out.

As she sat in the house, filling everyone in on how they'd met and tales of their journey across the country, she watched the men outside. While they sat drinking their coffee, Phoebe had a chance to hold the baby.

"Where's Eliza? I thought that's who Colton had said Reid had married." She noticed the others look to one another, then Ella answered.

"Eliza didn't survive childbirth. Reid's been raising Sophia on his own. Well, we've all been helping, but..." She shrugged as she reached out to touch her niece's soft hair.

Phoebe's heart broke as she looked out and understood the exact moment Reid shared the news with Colton. She knew Colton didn't have feelings for the other woman anymore and had confessed that he didn't think he ever really had. She'd been a way to get under his older brother's skin, who Colton felt blamed him for their father's death.

But she also understood Colton's guilt over leaving his brother the way they had. He would feel guilt that he hadn't been here to help when his brother had needed him.

After spending the day with the family, getting

to know them and letting them know they were here to stay, Phoebe and Colton were headed back to Bethany where the others had set up camp for the night.

She was surprised to realize she was actually looking forward to seeing the wagon and being back in the camp. She knew it was coming to an end and everyone would find their own places to stay for the winter, so she was anxious to be able to spend the night all together again.

Coming over the crest of a hill, she took in the beauty of the Willamette Valley. She breathed in deeply, feeling the crisp air hitting her lungs. She could see the few wagons of their outfit camped just on the outskirts of the town. Someone had already started a fire and she thought she could hear the sounds of a fiddle drifting up to her ears.

Colton pulled his horse in front of hers, stopping her. He jumped down from the saddle, then reached up for her.

"What are you doing?" She didn't know why he'd stopped.

He didn't say anything, just stood smiling up at her waiting for her to take his hands so he could help her down.

As she reached out her hand, he pulled her closer so he could grab her waist and swing her down. Holding her in front of him, he brought his lips down to hers. After kissing her until her knees felt like they would buckle, he lifted his head and smiled down at her.

"What was that for?" She could feel herself getting lost in the blue gaze that was holding her in place.

"Well, we're about to get back with all the others and I needed to have you to myself for just a moment more."

He moved her in front of him and they stood in silence, with his arms holding her close as they looked across the valley. The little settlement called Bethany was about to become her home.

"I will almost miss being on the trail. As difficult as it was, I am thankful to have gone through it with you."

"Even when I didn't agree with you?" She poked him in the ribs. "I'm pretty sure you spent most of the trip reminding me how much trouble I was."

"I'll admit, when I saw you trying to save those damn chickens from the storm, I could have strangled you." He tightened his arms around her as she tensed, ready to argue once more why she'd done that.

"But I also realized then that any woman who'd care that much about a couple of chickens was someone I would like to have in my life." He waited a few seconds before continuing. "Even if it did take me a few more weeks to let myself admit it."

Phoebe smiled as she turned to face Colton. He

reached up, touching the soft fabric of the bonnet he'd given her. "I love you, Phoebe Hamilton, even if you are a crazy woman who would risk her life to save a couple of chickens."

He lowered his head to hers and their lips met in a kiss full of promise. When they lifted their heads, she looked into the eyes she'd fallen so much in love with. "And I love you, Colton Wallace. Thank you for agreeing to take two stray girls along when you could have left us behind. Thank you for caring enough about Grace to risk your own reputation on the wagon train and giving her a chance to live. Thanks to you, I was able to keep my promise to my ma."

"Phoebe, I have no doubt you'd have found a way to get her to safety. I'm just glad that way was with me."

"Phoebe?" The sound of her sister's voice carried up to her. She turned and saw her walking up over the hill.

"What are you doing out here?" She was surprised to see her alone up on the hill.

"It's just so beautiful here. I had to take a look around." She was smiling and, Phoebe noticed, the smile made it all the way to her eyes. "I'm so glad we came."

"Well, this will be your home now, Grace." Colton smiled down at the young girl.

As Phoebe watched, her sister walked over to

Colton and threw her arms around him. "Thank you, Colton, for bringing us here."

She felt tears well up in her eyes as she realized how happy her sister was. Colton hugged the girl back, then pulled back and smiled down at her with one eyebrow raised. "You finally called me Colton."

Grace shrugged as she moved to stand beside Phoebe.

"Let's get down to the wagons and have some fun." Colton picked Phoebe up and set her on her horse, then hopped up on his, turning to lift Grace up with him. The smile he sent her direction tore right through to her heart and she realized, she'd found home.

AFTERWORD

I hope you enjoyed learning a bit more about the Oregon Trail. My story followed actual events and mention real landmarks from along the trail.

The fire in St. Louis that caused the death of Phoebe and Grace's father happened on May 17, 1849.

A paddle wheel steamboat called the "White Cloud" on the river caught fire, which quickly spread to other steamboats and barges. Sparks leaped to the shoreline, causing the buildings along the shore to catch fire which then spread and was finally contained after 11 hours.

When it was all over, 430 buildings were burned, 23 steamboats and more than 12 other boats were destroyed and at least 3 people had died, including a fire captain. (And, of course for the purpose of our story, one of those may very well have been Phoebe's father.)

During this time, there was also a cholera outbreak that killed many people, one of those being the mother of Phoebe and Grace.

TAKE A LOOK AT BOOK TWO: AUDREY'S AWAKENING

A marriage in name only...

After losing her husband on the Oregon Trail, Audrey is being forced to go back home and marry a man her father has chosen. Still grieving her husband, and not wanting to leave her new home in Oregon, she makes the decision to marry a man who needs her help looking after his daughter - *a marriage he has said will be in name only.*

Reid Wallace lost his wife during childbirth and has been raising his two-year-old daughter alone. His heart died with his wife, and he has vowed to never love again.

The new couple will go up against a father determined to have the marriage annulled and take her home, illness, insecurity, and guilt as their hearts struggle with the new feelings they are uncovering.

Will they be able to overcome everything that seems to be working to destroy the future they are building together? And can they help each other heal the pain in their hearts, while finding a way to love again?

AVAILABLE MARCH 2022

ABOUT THE AUTHOR

USA Today Bestselling Author, Kay P. Dawson writes sweet western romance – the kind that leaves out all of the juicy details and immerses you in a true, heartfelt love story. Growing up pretending she was Laura Ingalls, she's always had a love for the old west and pioneer times. She believes in true love, and finding your happy ever after.

Happily married mom of two girls, Kay has always taught her children to follow their dreams. And, after a breast cancer diagnosis at the age of 39, she realized it was time to take her own advice. She had always wanted to write a book, and she decided that the someday she was waiting for was now.

She writes western historical, contemporary and time travel romance that all transport the reader to a time or place where true love always finds a way.

Made in the USA
Las Vegas, NV
31 July 2022

52486744R00114